SPY THRILLER

THE SLEEPER SERIES

ONLY ONE REALITY THAT KILLS

By Anna Schlegel

BOOK FOUR

Translation from Russian

Schlegel Press Association

Only One Reality That Kills by Anna Schlegel
Book Four of The Sleeper Series

Published by Schlegel Press Association
Friedrichstr. 123
Berlin, Germany 10117

ISBN: 9780999127612

First Edition: June 2017

Translated by Alla Koshechkina
Cover photography by Shutterstock

"...The Sleeper Series is a modern, fast-paced spin on British Intelligence operations that offers an entirely different perspective on why intelligence people become defectors."

- MSNBC

"...spy novel, promising to unravel the tangled web of a strange couple caught in the middle of an espionage game of British intelligence."

- The Huffington Post

"...a thriller that begins with a couple's discussion about intelligence processes and evolves to a cat-and-mouse game played out across the streets of Europe."

- Midwest Book Review

Also By Anna Schlegel
THE SLEEPER SERIES

MONEY CAN'T LIE
Book One of The Sleeper Series
Should there be three pieces of crap, this is of the British Intelligence classic.

WHO SPREADS FOR WHOM
Book Two of The Sleeper Series
The British intelligence cannot compromise its integrity, it will adhere to its principles like in the old times of rock 'n' roll. And it's damn good to look at it working... but then it's scary to see it work against you.

THE GODS SMILE ON THE BASTARDS
Book Three of The Sleeper Series
Once you are able to see the intelligence's handwriting, you may see the words of failure inscribed in the same handwriting, telling of a failure they are yet unaware of.

LIE MAKES ME LIVE
Book Five of The Sleeper Series
This game of the intelligence, we were either to see through it, or die.
Coming soon

Also By Anna Schlegel
THE DEAD BANK DIARY SERIES

THE DEAD BANK DIARY
Book One of The Dead Bank Diary Series
The rats living on the refuse of the bank's backyard stay full at all time.

FOR THOSE IN THE SHADE
Book Two of The Dead Bank Diary Series
You may live your whole life without getting to know who you are, and sometimes this is for the better.

THE PRINTS ON THE SNOWS OF YESTERYEAR
Book Three of The Dead Bank Diary Series
The best one to rob the bank is the banker himself.

SOME DAY I'LL HIT A BANK
Book Four of The Dead Bank Diary Series
The bomb lives to its internal time.

THE FROZEN DEBT
Book Five of The Dead Bank Diary Series
When totally nude have a look, maybe you still have the shoulder loops.

CONTENTS

AUTHOR'S NOTE

What do the defectors really want? Why do these people betray their country and friends? Why are some of those defectors lucky, while some others are not? Why don't they ever have any regrets?

What are their true motives? Is it about money? No. Do they do it for fear? No. Do they sometimes wish to build their careers in this alternative way? No. Are they seeking fame? No. Have they been brainwashed? No. Can they be naive idealists? No.

Whatever answers you may think of, all of them would be probably wrong.

Are they betrayers? Yes, they are. Are they doing the right thing? Yes, they are. Do they find in this treachery what they must have been looking for? They sometimes do. How can they live with this? They are perfectly in tune with their own selves.

What are their goals? Now you will have the answer. It is worth knowing. This answer will surely change the way you see the world. This will be the answer from the legend.

It happens to everyone without exception. It will inevitably happen to you, unless you live under the wing of the legend.

ONLY ONE REALITY THAT KILLS

He was back. No one believed it was him until he started killing those who had no more doubts.

ABOUT THE SLEEPER SERIES

Each of the secret services has its own handwriting, faint and hardly perceptible. This handwriting is their custom. It does not change for years, and one can read it through. This handwriting can lead an agent to failure. This is what these books are written about, if anything.

These books also tell of the legend that keeps recruiting people across time and distance; of something that is stronger than life. This legend is an eternal truth, refilled with the living blood of every new recruiter who would choose the way of the legend. These books are about the legendary Kim Philby.

These books contain neither facts of Kim Philby's life nor any historical events. This is all about the modern-day, and is pure fiction.

I'm giving an answer to the question: Why should the legend of Philby be everlasting? Why is this legend of Philby such a deadly, pulling force? How do the people survive under the wing of his legend?

There is little said about it, yet this is the main point.

They become traitors long before they step across the threshold of the spy directorate. They step across expressly to turn into traitors one fine day. That is the way they see their careers. They wish to re-act that life of the icon. The legend of Kim Philby makes them traitors from the moment they open that book of his or read about him. This legend keeps recruiting people without money or contracts. The reality is forceless against it. The legend keeps dictating its own logic. It may come along imperceptibly. Once the book of the legend is read through and half-forgotten, it sprouts deep inside and lives to its own time, so one day it will casually remind of its existence, in an implicit way, and push its follower to make the decision which he must have prepared for long ago, when an occasion was in short supply.

Most paradoxically, such agents appear to be more mature, and do not really care much about public recognition, awards, money, appreciation, and all those matters connected with a regular, rewarding career. They do not really fall for the uniform and regalia. Surely, the traitors get incomparably better money, but it was not always this way, and would never be the main point. These people rate themselves so highly that money does not measure that value. They are, essentially, free.

For such people, there is no borderline where they become traitors; they must have since long slipped across by taking no notice. These people are usually well-educated and highbrow, and, as such, intelligently cruel and deeply calculating.

They are idealists. The philosophy of theirs makes blood turn to ice. This is how the legend of Kim Philby works. And it's a damn good British job.

CHAPTER ONE

NEVER TRUST ANYONE

Zehlendorf, Monday, 21 February 2011, around 09.00 p.m.

The States might request them to give him up. It was time to escape.

I could imagine Vlad and me walking out onto the house porch, prickly powder snow dusting my frozen face and my fingers freezing, then standing there on the porch for a few moments that would seem too long, the darkness around us sticky like snow and getting under my scarf to my very neck, burning my skin. We had no idea where to flee.

We could go to another similar house in pledge with the same bank at the other end of Berlin, also abandoned and empty, and we would find it equally warm in there. But could we really hide away? This time it was about the Russian intelligence being constrained to sell Ivan out to the States.

Ivan was no more there. He was not the kind of person to be easily found, even given the efforts of the secret services. But did they really need to search for him? Whom could they start looking for if, most probably, Ivan's case file had been bought out and destroyed? He was a ghost of his own self; a mere nobody. He could, now, have any kind of identity paperwork and whatever life he wanted. He only *resembled* Vlad. And that was the trouble. Ivan and Vlad looked similar; like the Kray Twins.

Ivan had taken the name with which Vlad was born and which he used for twenty years in San Francisco, when he was recruited by Ivan. Ivan had now made his appearance as Harvey Smith. That is why Vlad could no longer have this name, along with this past of his. Vlad actually felt it as a burden now, as Smith at this point appeared to be a random small coin in the game of several secret service agencies. It was not his game. And those guys seemed ready to give him up any minute now.

With every move in this weird chess game, Vlad turned out to be a mere figurehead that each of the players was eager to sacrifice without much thought. Ivan had assumed the role of that piece for a short while. Ivan had tried to prove that he was, himself, that very figurehead, Harvey Smith. And he'd proven damn convincing, as such. He'd told them everything they must have wanted to hear, without raising any suspicion. Hardly anyone, gazing at Ivan, would think that the man was not the true Smith. Why did they require this Smith? What reason could they possibly have, now that everything had been spoken out loud – now that the banker Schuman, against whom the Americans had been about to bring charges of espionage, would no longer come to the courtroom? So, why? Ivan had been asked a lot of questions. He'd given replies to almost all of them, with only one exception. But at that time, we had no idea.

Ivan must have told them when and by whom he'd been recruited. By giving the codename of his boss in Moscow; he must have told them that the companies where he used work as an auditor had been buying up Russia's foreign debts, scattering them around to all sorts of private hands as debt securities. He must have told them that he'd been reporting to his spymaster regarding the amounts that these companies received for buyup purposes, and how many of those bills had been bought out. This was not real espionage; it was, rather, a regular financial scheme. But then, the point might have been the money, couldn't it?

Ivan had left of his own accord – or they could have allowed him to go. One way or another, he was there no more. Instead, the Russians could give out Vlad's dead body. It was silly to think the story would turn out some other way. Such things had happened before.

And then, Vlad had seen the British intelligence work from up close... Holy shit, could Vlad have been working for the British, too? This flashed through my mind, and I found it hard to get it out of my head.

I looked at Vlad, and I could see him through the lines in the book of Dr. Norman.

They became traitors long before they started to work for the spy directorate. The legend of Kim Philby made them traitors from the moment they opened that book of his. They stepped across the threshold with the sign "You will know the truth, and the truth will set you free," expressly to turn into traitors one fine day. They had no idea of having long since chosen their career path. A mere opportunity turned them into traitors. No lie detector would be able to spot them; such people live in harmony with and never blame themselves. And they unknowingly wished to reenact the life of the icon. The legend kept recruiting people without money or contracts, across time and distance. It is an everlasting illusion; the reality is forceless against it. It is stronger than life, as the legends sucks the fresh blood of yet another human that may choose the way of the legend.

The legend makes them idealists. And the philosophy of theirs turns blood into ice. It is better to remain unaware of it; not to destroy the traditional concepts of life and beliefs. These people are like living bombs. That is how the legend works. And that is a damn good British job.

I could see the ghost of Kim Philby behind Vlad's back as clearly as if I could touch it with my hand.

Whatever Vlad told me now, I would not be able to believe him.

This is what I felt until I saw a message on my cell phone screen that read: *they may request that Smith be given out to the States.* Then, all these truths and lies turned to be penny-wise and meaningless. At that particular moment I did not really care who Vlad really was, and for whom he could have been working. I just wanted him to stay alive.

Vlad only told me,

"Haven't I told you before that you should never trust anyone? Very good, mein herz, I see that you really hear me."

Vlad said this not for the first time. As per his words, too many things could turn out to be a mere illusion.

"You should not believe in my being murdered until you can feel a bullet in my corpse with your own fingers. You should not believe I`m dead unless you see my corpse in the mortuary. Look, I've got a scar under my chin; that's why I don't fancy shaving so much ... You should make sure it's truly me. And don't you believe in anything. You will get used to thinking just like me. You'd better do so sooner than later; otherwise, you won't be able to survive."

Sure enough, I could see that the British Intelligence covered up for Vlad, and Vlad could see this, too. One had to be blind not to notice a delicate move through which defunct manager Vlad Holt had replaced Vlad, so the suspicion was diverted from him in his role as businessman Andreas Leman. A few more details, and Leman had become a common business person; an involuntary copy of Smith, due to their amazing facial resemblance.

Ivan had told them how he had managed to obtain Leman's passport in the first place; and then of that of Holt. Vlad had told me the same story from the very beginning. At that time, over twenty years ago, they used to find in the police records a similar-looking person who'd long since left the country, so they just changed the photo. After some time the person in question might come back from abroad, pay a visit to the police office, and report his passport lost. Later on, the man would be issued a new, legitimate passport with his own photo. Well, this was about identity theft, but it had nothing to do with the secret services. It was a police case.

As to Smith, he was mainly handled by the British Intelligence. Why was he of any interest to the British? We'd observed the interchange of the suspects for a whole month, with suspicion diverted from one person to another, and saw the paperwork resurface then disappear. We kept looking at this wonderful work, and found it breathtaking. Vlad could clearly see every move, and his fear was mixed with admiration. But the stakes in this game went higher, so the British services seemed eventually constrained to play for the higher stakes, and thus supplied the living Harvey Smith.

Was it so that this living witness could do better than a dead one? So that he could tell everyone of his San Francisco experience twenty years back? We did not believe it until Ivan came forward. He told them everything, including his memories of the blackberry pancakes. He remembered San Francisco so well. He loved his home city and kept longing for it, and they could see this.

Then we clearly realized how important this Smith was. Why so? Could he really have been working for the British? That was my initial guess; but at this particular moment, I had a different idea.

There is no such thing as gratitude in this world. That is why so many ex-agents eventually get exposed. They usually file a lawsuit against their ex-employers and the trials follow, one after another. Such lawsuits must not have started just yesterday. When in court, one simple thing became clear over and over again: you would never get paid, and no one would ever take care of you, the hell they need you. No one is really interested in loyalty, honor and chores – all that the young boys come with, only to leave later on as embittered and poverty-stricken old men. This happened to everyone. The same happens to defectors. They start filing lawsuits. And they get some payment for a while, but then they are usually thrown out like garbage. What could be a source of income for a retired agent, really? The kind of old stuff they keep in their memories, which are no longer good even for the flea market? Hardly so.

Vlad had been given a cover, as they probably still needed him as a backup for Ivan – that is, either alive or dead. Until this point we'd believed that the British still needed Vlad alive, for some damn reason. We just wished to believe it, and the mere detail that Vlad was still alive reconfirmed the same. But Vlad was mistaken, there. He considered himself to be Harvey Smith, covered up by two other duplicates. True, the situation actually looked to be that way. Smith had been covered up because there was Ivan, acting as Smith. In fact, they must have provided Ivan with two backup men; one of whom was Vlad operating as Harvey Smith himself, under the name of Andreas Leman. What did it feel like to find out that you were nothing more than a duplicate of your own self? That is: a piece they would part with without any regrets, as soon as the need arose. Ivan appeared to be more important to preserve: he was a deep cover agent and a spymaster for the Russian group. Vlad remained just Andreas Leman, an involuntary duplicate for Ivan, who also held the passport of Leman.

I still called him Vlad. But he could no longer bear this name of Vlad Holt. I had the name of Vlada Holt, and my marriage certificate. Vlad Holt, the kind of Vlad had been playing, was now dead. Vlad used to have the name with which he was born, earlier; that of Harvey Smith. It no longer belonged to him, either. Ivan had turned into Harvey Smith. Vlad still had the name Andreas Leman. But then, could he still have it? No, he could not really have it anymore.

True, damn it: actually, Vlad had arranged for that passport of Vlad Holt on his own behalf, while the passport of Leman had been given to him by a Russian liaison agent. It appeared to be a highly reliable passport. How could Vlad know there were two similar passports issued in the name of Leman? One of them was designated for Ivan and another one for him, so that he could pass as a backup man for Ivan.

And what about Vlad Holt's passport, then? Vlad had arranged for that one right away, soon after his arrival to Berlin. It had probably become known, and it had been enough for Ivan to visit the police office and report his passport lost, again. This way, another passport in the name of Vlad Holt must have landed in Ivan's hands. So Vlad, with Holt's passport, once again had become a duplicate for Ivan, just like the real Vlad Holt; the man since long living in New York.

Vlad knew that such things happened, but when this happened to him, he was not ready for it. He was crushed. No matter how many cases there might have been before the same thing happened to you, you would still think it was someone else's case, and that other man must have been not smart enough, or maybe was too greedy, or that he must have made a mistake. You would never expect the same thing could happen to you; you would still have hope.

In a similar way that legal proceedings against captured defectors are usually viewed, the people around them can see their mistakes, but it seems like no one would ever make a similar mistake; that you could be far more cautious and smarter...

Indeed, there arose a lot of defectors after such proceedings, and all of them must have learned from the mistakes of their predecessors, as the next wave of defectors seemed somewhat more prudent and smarter... Surely they were all more cautious and smarter; but they were eventually caught anyway, and festered behind bars. In fact, nothing much really depended on their prudence and brain power, including the brightest, the smartest, and the most talented men. All of them ended up being given away by some other defector. They were given away by the people they trusted, or by those who knew all about them in their official capacity. They were given away by traitors, and it will be so forever. They were given away by the secret services for which they worked, and they were given away by their new masters. One cannot really step into the barnyard without getting poop all over.

Vlad had told me... I could not remember the exact wording, but I could recollect him saying something like, *It'll be that way only, unless you live under the wing of the legend.*

And that time it seemed to me, for a moment, that there was no ghost standing behind Vlad's back; but Vlad was standing behind the back of the ghost.

Fine: now we could very well forget the mere trifles, like Vlad being wanted alive.

The Russians only wanted Vlad dead. If that was so, then, even if it was otherwise, he would be killed and would be kept in a freezer, just like Vlad Holt, somewhere near at hand, in case Ivan's dead body was required. Indeed, they might need it one day. Where could Ivan be, at this time? To my mind, Ivan was now somewhere far away. To all appearances, they must have reached an understanding that, after completing this single task, Ivan was free to go to the four winds. Ivan was free, now: it appeared difficult to locate him with no trace. Even if he was found, who could ever tell it was him, really? Wouldn't it be a lot easier to say, by looking at the dead body of Vlad, that: *Yes, that's him, he was Smith twenty years ago, recruited by the Russian;, and then one fine day he turned up at the lawyer's office with a Russian passport, as Ivan Ivanov.*

And where could he escape from the Russian intelligence? Surely he could have a run. But for how long could it last, if no one really was interested in keeping him alive anymore?

It flashed through my mind that I had to make a call to Hoffman and tell him that Vlad had been Harvey Smith, give him the full story, and then ask him for help. That was silly. I guessed that Hoffman had been since long aware of Vlad's true personality. The best thing was that Vlad as Smith was of no interest to anyone. Why would they need him, if the role of Harvey Smith had been so well performed by Ivan? After his performance, Vlad, in this role of Smith, could only look like a provincial actor. Vlad was of no value to anyone any longer. As a dead man, well, maybe; but he was no longer wanted alive.

Even if Hoffman agreed to help him out and managed to send Vlad to prison some place, the Russians would carry him out chopped into pieces, pack him in a bag, and then give him away. The Russians would not spoil the relationship with the American side over such a minor issue as a long-forgotten agent. The American side probably wanted to get Smith alive, but they could hardly hope for more than his dead body. This dead body would be a polite and safe enough favor.

Or could Vlad possibly pay yet another visit to the US Embassy and tell them all? Then his dead body would be discovered right there. The Russians would not give up Smith in any format – neither him, nor Ivan – because this Smith could start talking and tell them something different than what he really knew. No one, including Vlad and me, had any doubts regarding just one point: this Vlad knew nothing at all and was of no value for anyone, any longer. Ivan had rescued Vlad by means of depreciating him, but at the same time, he'd set him to zero.

So there was a risk that Smith could start talking about things he did not really know; something he would be promoted to tell.

"Get ready fast; let us go," Vlad ordered me, folding his paperwork and whatever came under his hand, putting it into the sink, and setting it on fire. "Take the laptop and the discs with the press articles. Could you also help me with packing things that need washing up?" he requested.

"Do you want to do the laundry? Right now?"

"Yes, I'd rather leave no smell."

We hung the washed clothes and the bed linen, and I had time enough to clean the floor and everywhere else my hands could reach. I could hear Vlad washing the dishes and the spoons clinking in the kitchen that now seemed empty. Vlad switched off the fridge and dumped the remaining foodstuffs and everything else he could find into a waste bag, leaving just the coffee; then he packed his backpack and made us each a cup of coffee, then tucked the coffeemaker away into a carton box. There were only two cups of coffee on the table.

We took a seat at the table, and I asked him,

"Where are we heading to?"

"No idea."

Vlad usually had an answer to any question, and one day I'd made a joke that I would never hear from him the words like: *no idea*. If I'd only known that I would hear these words from him, *no idea,* in these circumstances.

We walked out onto the porch and the darkness lit my eyes. The cramped courtyard between the abandoned houses was filled with darkness to the flaky roofs, and the old poplar trees seemed to blend into this blackness, as if they were underwater. The house behind us pulled us in with the warmth of its rooms and the smell of cigarette smoke. For the split second we lingered on the porch, we could feel the time of eternity invisibly pass by, hidden in this darkness. The prickly snow instantly powdered my face, and my fingers were about to turn to ice. Vlad rolled up his scarf, put up his coat collar, and tucked his hands into his pockets. I could see the snow stick into his hat, scarf, and the bristle on his face and bite into his face, which was whiter than usual. He looked confused. We had no idea where to flee.

"When I'm about to get killed, I feel so damn alive. It's exciting," Vlad said, walking off the porch.

As we entered into the depth of the courtyard, we could feel the ice crust break under our feet and it carried the glasslike clink and chilly echo away into the depth of the empty buildings.

CHAPTER TWO

THE SMELL OF MEN

Berlin, Hoffmann's office, February 2011

Ivan had given the name that Nick wanted to hear, Todd Miller. In his mansard flat, with a bottle of beer, Nick kept casting about in his mind the names of the people able to find out what the man could be busy with. And he failed to define such person.

Todd Miller. Yes, at this point Nick had actually heard this name from a different person. Ivan could do fine as a witness, but where could they possibly search for him now? And what if this was a frame-up?

Nick suspected five different employees of the Agency, but he actually believed that Todd Miller was the mole. Why so? He could not tell it for sure but some kind of gut feeling hinted him that it was Miller.

He's got a feeling that he could not have detected Miller on his own, that someone must have been feeding him this Miller. True, it was his own conclusion that Miller was the mole, but had not it been too easy for him to detect the man?

He recollected Miller and his bowed back, his dry-skin yellow pinky face with a forward gray chin, his parrot nose and his red eyes under the bright pink transparent eyelids, and his prickly glance.

Nick picked up his cell phone several times, speaking to himself, *He's gone, I'm sorry, Stan ... Hi, Stan, I've lost the man...I've let him slip by, I understand it all...* and then, after dialing the number he heard him say, *You've lost the man.*

Anyway, at this point Ivan was not the main concern. It was high time to interrogate Miller. Whether this Miller was a mole or not, once the internal investigation started against Miller, everyone who was still in disbelief regarding this search for the Russian insider would finally get to believe in it, and then there was a chance that the mole could somehow manifest himself.

After this conversation Nick gave a call to Hoffmann and told him that the situation had grown out of control, that the cupcake had managed to create an impression, and that the States might wish to request the delivery of Ivan from Moscow. He listened to the silence of Hoffmann, as if the man was speaking to him. Then finally Hoffmann uttered,

"You'll get a dead Leman instead of a live Ivan, in a refuse bag, most probably. I hope you understand this. Leman will stay in my house, and he will be guarded by my own people. Would you be so kind to make it the way this delivery never takes place? If you can't, you'll be all by yourself over here. And it won't last for long. And the best outcome would be – they pull you from handling this case and call you off."

By hanging off Nick realized that he must have made a mistake. He was supposed to bring Schumann down in a discreet way, if possible. Any kind of scandal would have played into Schumann's hand. Berlin was his territory. He dialed Hoffmann's number again and said,

"Ernest, you are right. We cannot really get this Ivan... alive. But we've still got his copy. Could we have a talk and share a bottle of beer?"

Zehlendorf, February 2011, Monday 21, around 10.00 p.m.

Why had Ivan so handily turned up? The answer was clear. Whoever he worked for, in the first place, he worked for the best interests of the Russian secret services. This meant that he must have stepped in not to ruin the whole trial against the banker Martin Schumann. Above everything else, he'd stepped in to protect his former Russian group, for which he used to be a spymaster. It was also to protect Vlad, as Vlad used to be one of his people.

Vlad had been sure that Ivan was doing his term in prison, or had died by now. Where could Ivan have been for these twenty years? What could he have been doing? He'd probably had no rest on pension, as he'd spoken as if he was ready to answer the lawyers' questions, everything fresh and bright in his memory, so he couldn't be someone no longer involved in the matter.

Had this Schumann just incidentally found himself at the intersection of several parties' interests? Or could he have actually provoked this intersection himself, to keep his own balance? We believed that there was a lot of circumstance to this story. In fact, the only witness able to confirm that Schumann had been recruited twenty years ago and then forgotten was Smith, the man who'd been working by his side for the same firm.

It initially appeared enough for this trial to have a dead man, Smith; but then a living Smith had stepped in. Wasn't this enough? It was probably not enough to explain something more like a bomb explosion that had happened in Langley, which probably had something to do with the same Russian group and also with Smith. This was our understanding of this intersection. Ivan must have explained everything, but we did not know what, exactly, he had told them; we could only guess. Anyway, something must have remained unsaid — something very important, if there were now talks that this Smith was being requested to give away to the States.

Surely Ivan could have been working for the British side, also; there must have been some kind of agreement. Ivan was probably supposed to handle the issues of the banker Schumann, meanwhile providing the cover for the British source … And what could their source be, damn it? Ivan seemed equally determined to resolve his own issues.

But what were they, exactly? They must have been incomparably more serious, provided he'd taken so much risk. What could they be?

Vlad thought that Ivan had to cover up for a certain leak.

The sense of guilt noticed by Richter, an old friend of Vlad – the guilt that everyone around could also notice just by looking at Ivan – was probably not due to the man's remorse for his people. Ivan's men, whoever had worked for him in those years, were able to walk away and must have been scattered around the world, probably, unsuspecting of the fact that someone had recollected them, just the same as Vlad. Ivan would hardly worry about his backup men or about the dummies that had been arrested. All of them had been trained to do their job, and they did just fine. They all survived.

Ivan was probably concerned about someone else; someone who was not ready to face prison, whose arrest could entail major losses. He probably worried about the mole on the verge of exposure. Otherwise, the whole story made no sense. His task must have been to either provide protection for the mole and divert suspicion from him, or pull him out. Otherwise... This is how Vlad saw it.

As we walked down the boulevard that embraced the flow of highway lights with a black wall and failed to hold it, the light splashed across the illuminated house windows and the strings of lights on the trees along the sidewalk, pouring into the windows of the convenience stores and playing in the reflections of café windows. Our faces, caught in the streetlamp light, white and merging with the snow stuck to the coat, flashed by in the shop reflection where I used to buy the mini cakes. I thought: *We wanted so much to get out of that house of ours, missing the point that once we were out, we would have nowhere to go.*

"Otherwise... What else could it be, there? What could it be?" I kept asking him, covering my face from the snow.

"A dead mole is always way better than a living one... Wait. No." Vlad slackened his pace.

Why was Vlad thinking about it? With great tenacity he kept spinning the idea that could be just a wild guess of his. He wanted to follow it to its logical end. I could see no logic, though. From the viewpoint where I could only see the precipice stretching up and beyond the horizon, Vlad could forecast yet another move for the downfall. To him, it seemed a sort of a chess game. He could see a variety of possible moves, and then opted for something that seemed the easiest to make; the most evident one. This way, by now, he had arrived at the conclusion a few times that he would turn into a dead body. He seemed to step away and look at it from a distance, then lit a cigarette, had another look, and left it again.

"No. It's not the thing. I started thinking about myself. I'm a pawn. A pawn that always gets killed so that a major piece can survive. They only sacrifice the latter, if worse comes to worst. So let us consider it not the last resort, but a regular case. Then, the suspicion is usually diverted from the major piece to someone else. And if that other person is dead, the move turns out to be not good enough. This can be quickly forecasted. So they probably would divert suspicion to some other major piece; someone of equal value. If that other piece is given away to the counterintelligence, they would accept it and say: *Thanks*. And that piece would survive."

"And we would never be able to find out anything about them, as there would be no death notice. You actually come to play with two unknown variables. Only Ivan knows them both, but he must be far away, now. Those are the issues of Ivan and the Russian side. It hardly has anything to do with us."

"Fine, let us forget all about it for the time being," Vlad agreed.

We stopped to brush the snow from our collars and hats, then started to smoke. We were in no hurry. We had nowhere to rush, did we? We walked on, hiding our cigarettes under palms that were freezing up with the snow, which kept falling and biting our faces.

"Vlad, how can you still think about it?!"

"I wish I could simply take my mind off it. What else can I do there? Or should I pity myself? Just think, damn you: could you mollify me with some kind of nonsense? Don't you tell me you've got no more stuff in store!"

"What about Schumann? Will he walk away just like that? After this entire story?"

"He would not really walk away. As the case was getting ready for trial, we could still see something through Richter's eyes. Right now we'll have to play it blind. Shit, I hate playing blind. Why is there always that kind of crap? Where do I get it from, down onto my head? As if a whole sewage conduit has broken through ... Wait. No. It's not about my sewer full of shit. I've just been pelted a little bit, as well as

Schumann. It must have broken through in Langley. This is where they've got the most of that shit. If only we knew where it comes from and what kind of shit it is, exactly?"

"We've got several pieces of crap. Why the fuck has Ivan turned up? In what way would the Americans choose to finish off Schumann? What could that twenty-year old crap have been?"

We had discussed it a thousand times. We had no clue. How could Ivan have disappeared? He was probably getting tracked.

"He must have left with Leman's passport," Vlad somewhat echoed. "When I was about to quit San Francisco, I already knew that Ivan would live under my name. He had to stay there somehow, with whatever identity. Later on, I was given this passport of Leman – a highly reliable passport, as it turned out. They must have checked me through to my trunks. I guess that with the consideration that Ivan was supposed to continue living with that face of mine, they must have made us two passports in the name of Leman; one for me and one for him. And thus, Ivan has also taken from me the name of Andreas Leman."

Vlad seemed to finally understand what was underway; he stopped and turned me around to face him.

"Vlada, listen to me! Sooner or later Ivan will turn up again. I don't want you to mix us up. Please take a good look at me, now."

Keeping in mind Vlad's words, I unwillingly focused on a hardly visible scar under his chin and then right away waved aside all this bullshit. I did not have to look at him to make sure it was him. Now, looking straight into Vlad's eyes, I thought that he simply wanted to have another look at me, as if he was telling me goodbye.

He had a white face and cheeks blushed with the biting frost, featuring white bristle and white eyebrows and eyelashes. His temples, touched with gray, seemed a patch of never-melting snow on his face, with his delicate weather-beaten skin in hardly visible freckles. His eyes, pale, frozen, and transparent like ice, deadly condescending, were gone, now. Vlad looked so handsome, like... there seemed both a youngster and a man in him, and a damn lot of sex appeal combined with the calculating power of an expensive whore. Whatever he was wearing, be it his well-used woolen jacket stretching across his broad, crooked shoulders or wornout jeans, one could see from afar that he was someone with a high price, but still available for sale. He was what you call a genuine bastard.

I could see it so very well – maybe way too well. I used to be a trader, and I was accustomed to men looking at me to give an eyeball estimate, as if I were a thing on sale. I used to see my price in their eyes; I knew to let them understand, with a single look, how much I cost. I used to see a man contemplate, when looking at me, whether he was ready to part with his money. However high that price of mine, I was still for sale. I used to sell myself again and again. It was the law of the market where I lived. In fact, it was not me, as such, on sale; it was more about what I brought along with me - it was about a deal proposal. I never agreed to a sleepover without a ready deal. If the man I came to see with a deal proposal was ready to handle it and paid me commission fees, he was also entitled to have me as a bonus. Otherwise, I did my best to keep away from such men. It was long time back. When recollecting my crazy life in the stock market, I could only think, *How could I have been so smart?* No, I was just a good trader, rather hardnosed; with the same kind of damn tough mind as Vlad.

In fact, I had no chance to find out that there existed another kind of men. Ilya was this kind. Ilya must have bought me, too. When one day I'd found myself totally moneyless, ready to sell myself for whatever price to just about anyone, and then got sick, in had stepped Ilya, chairperson of a minor bank. He'd paid my annual apartment rent in Moscow, carried me to his country house, and called a doctor for me. For the whole week that followed he had not gone to his bank; he'd stayed with me and cooked me food. So, I ultimately felt happy with him.

For quite a long time I considered it a folly of his. Why would a seventy-year-old banker want a trader? At that time I was around forty, while he could have any long-legged young broker from the front office who was at his disposal. Ilya surely made a pretty good use of them. He still had a strong desire; the kind that brokers had. For quite a while it seemed to me that I was a mere toy to Ilya. After ten years, I still found it hard to believe in my relationship with Ilya, despite us being so similar; as if we both used to wee into the same potty when kids.

If not for Ilya, I would at this point rather remember myself as an expensive whore. Without him I would have since long become a cheap whore. I could often see my own future in the eyes of my clients, who had everything for sale: gold mines, bank guarantees, development work requests for a thousand tons of oil or a military equipment park... yet, they had no cash to pay for a metro ticket.

Ilya only observed that rat race of mine from afar; but if not for Ilya, I would have never known my cost.

Surely the price of Vlad, who was in charge of buying up some African countries' foreign debts, the deal so many wished to join in, was incomparably higher. Would I be able to replace him? Vlad couldn't go out on the street – it was a high risk – but still, someone had to see the partners, as some of them wanted to make sure that everything was fine by just glancing at Vlad from a distance. As per Vlad's words, they could read the message from his gait and know that something had gone wrong. So how could I possibly replace him?

I had tried doing it. Now I looked the same as Vlad: a blonde with a short haircut and pale eyebrows. Just recently, wearing the same hat Vlad used to wear and in a similar coat, with the round dim mirror glasses that Vlad used to wear for a walk, I'd passed by one of the partners who had requested an appointment with Vlad and had discreetly given him a nod from afar. How could I have acquired that much confidence, the same as Vlad? I'd seen those partners look at him, as if touching him with their looks, Vlad transmitted his confidence on to them as if through a handshake.

One day I'd noticed Vlad looking at me as if I were a piece he planned on selling at a good price. And I'd thought, *You're a profiteer, cupcake.*

Had we had sex with Vlad? Hmm... Vlad and I were, rather, like two whores locked up together: we could understand each other without words. It took us some time to get to value each other. No one is able to do it right away; people need time – a lot of time – to realize that the person living beside them is of endless value ... that is, not for someone ready to purchase him, but for you. One day you get to realize that you are ready to pay everything you have for him, even that life of yours. And the man is absolutely worth it.

Vlad was fucked up over these days. He'd said, *That's because I'm such a damn beauty.* With everything that happened... I found it hard to understand what was underway.

Looking into Vlad's eyes now was the same as seeing my own self in the mirror, where I could not read anything but fear.

How could I have got so attached to him? No. I could now see something else in him. Initially I feared seeing something similar to my own self in him; this caught my eyes right away. Just like me, Vlad appeared to have nine lives and was not picky, as a rat. Vlad was fond of Nietzsche. He had a metaphysical mindset: that is, he was able to cerebrate in such an abstract way that this whole world seemed to exist just in his imagination. No, not quite in his imagination — I was able to see through it and read him like a book. No matter what the book was about. It was probably different to every reader, but its single name was "My Silent War".

"Now, look at me!"

Vlad had a reason. Richter, once he'd seen Ivan, almost believed he was looking at Vlad in there, even though he was well aware it was someone else, not Vlad — the gait was different and the traits were somewhat more gnarly. Ivan was older, and one could see it; but then, Ivan also had all that charm and sex. As per Richter, *He'd had them all there*. For how long had Richter been looking at Ivan while the man kept answering all those lawyers' questions, taking his tea with a mini cake? For one hour? Or for a couple of hours? Richter had actually started to fear losing him.

"Forget it, Vlad. I would never mix you up with anyone else. I recognize men by their smells. I don't have to look at you to know that's really you."

"And what's Ilya's smell?"

"It's hard to tell right away, but Ilya always smells of snow. Victor smells of cheap smoke, and then he's also got that after-rain smell of the raw soil; this odor is always on him. Marc smells of the bonfire. My father smells of spring decay and stale leaves kept all winter under the snow."

I was fond of Marc's smell most of all. It was the smell of the bonfire and of home. Of course, Marc smelled of alcohol even stronger. He kept drinking gin for breakfast and supper. I could catch this smell from the doorstep, when Marc was about to enter the house. He was also fond of grilling over an open flame. It was the best, most peaceful smell on earth. Marc was a friend and a bodyguard of Ilya. Marc was always somewhere by his side, and with him being there, it was not that I feared nothing; but that I always felt at home. It must have taken Marc a while to get used to me. Ilya had been living alone for a long time. Once Marc had told me that he would not last forever; that someday he might be gone, and he would wish Ilya to still have someone. It would be good if I could be that very person.

After recollecting Ilya, I thought that, in true fact, people don't really need so much. I had a single friend who would remain with me for my whole life. I didn't really want to bring back to memory things about him at this point, but I'd really found it hard to leave him. There was one person who would rescue me, if it was still possible, and gun me down in case there was no chance of rescuing me. It was Marc. Then, after all, you need just a single man. It was Ilya. Surely, there were times when I had that wish to fuck the world around. I no longer wished this. I was lucky to have met him; the man who'd become for me that very person. And fuck if I ever lose him. I would get back to him, as I'd left to make my way back. Somewhere deep inside, this idea was phrased with the wording, *If I get back to him as a different person, would he be able to recognize me?* If only Ilya had patience enough to wait for me.

"What kind of a smell have I got?" Vlad asked me with curiosity.

"I can't really tell. It must be like hot wind along with sand dust."

"Ivan could do to you the same thing as he's done to Richter. You would be afraid of losing him."

How could he have managed to do it to Richter? Richter could easily do the same to just about anyone. When parting from Richter last time, I'd thought I could no longer meet him, as he pulled me in like a magnet and was able to do anything he wanted to me. I was powerless to resist him.

Vlad said that Ivan would not really come without a cause. At present, Ivan was far away; but one day he could return.

"Ivan is a friend, but if one day he turns up by your side for any reason whatsoever – that means he's become an enemy. If he ever turns up by your side, it means that he is interested in that business of ours; or maybe in one of the partners in the business. That would be the only reason."

"What am I supposed to do, then?" I asked him, still not quite clear about what Vlad was telling me.

"You'll have to kill him."

"What?" I must have misheard him because of the wind.

"Has Ilya got a bodyguard, or someone?"

"Yes, that's Marc. The one who smells of bonfire."

"Who is he?"

"I can't tell you now. You've taught me to be cautious."

One day I'd looked at Marc and realized that I had been given a rare opportunity to have an insight into my own soul. It was rather scary, and it was scary indeed to find out that Marc was that kind of person. Once I'd heard his laugh echo a thousand times, carried from one wall to another with the wind blowing through the iron hangar, howling in there like in an empty tube: an absolutely crazy laugh broken into several voices like in a mental clinic corridor, and it made me calm down. He was just like my own essence. Marc was sitting there in front of me, drinking his gin and smoking, and I could see the reflection of his cigarette lighter dance in his eyes. Not everyone can get an insight on his nature and realize what he truly is, deep inside.

Fortunately, I had never tried to push away what I came to understand; neither run away nor brush it aside. I was used to accepting everything that life could give me as a gift, and being thankful for whatever it was. It's a widely known message from the popular psychology that I'd never read. In a word, you are supposed to accept everything that comes to you because if you refuse, there might follow no other gifts, or there could be some that were not quite the kind you wished for, and not in good time. We do change, and our fate follows us with a slight delay so it may retain all those wishes we made many years ago and offer us things much wished for at some other point in the past. It may be needed no more, and many people refuse.

But then, if you still accept whatever is not really needed, fate may fulfill another wish of yours somewhat faster. It can give you something you really want, and they say that some people get their wishes fulfilled and synchronized to the minute. This was probably the case with Ilya. He didn't usually need money, and he never had to run after money, as he knew that he could take it any time. It was enough for him to stretch out his hand, and he would not even look at from whom he could take it. He'd once told me of having cleared the accounts of the Russian Federal Security Service one fine day, and since the money had been already brought into requisition, the Central Bank had been constrained to open a credit line for Ilya. Ilya had not become any more prudent or cautious since; not at all. He was the kind of person of whom people call a 'lucky devil'.

Right now, Ilya at seventy-five looked tall, highbred, and perfectly schooled. With all that, he was able to resolve all his issues as a broker without thinking at all. Unable to hold back, I'd once told him, *You're a whore, Ilya.* He'd responded, *True, I've given full satisfaction to all. To my regret, the head of the Central Bank is no female. It's hard to give him a proper fuck.*

Ilya had never brought his bank to a prominent position. He always kept to the shade, being rather cautious.

"You should call Marc, if you see Ivan somewhere nearby."

"Is Ivan on the Russian side?" I wondered.

Vlad said that I failed to understand a damn thing in there, again. Ivan was, above anything else, on his own side. He would initially pull his people out of the shit, and then he could take some time to think of which side he could hold on to. It was convenient for us to think that people were blinded by their principles or were brainwashed just because they held onto a different side. They could eventually join any side, if they found one of the parties had a grain of truth.

Vlad said this as if he was there than long ago, and I was left alone in that future without him.

"Vlad, don't you speak to me as if you are not there anymore? Could Victor give us a hint, maybe?" I quickly inserted the SIM card into my old cell. "Ilya has given me a message that you may be requested by the States — that is, Victor should know something."

My cell shivered in my hand, showing a text from Hoffmann, *I'm waiting for both of you in the same café right now.*

"Shall we go?" I asked Vlad.

He nodded, and we quickened the pace.

CHAPTER THREE

DELIRIUM

Berlin, Monday 21st, about 11 p.m.

We came to meet Hoffmann in a café opposite the lawyer's office where I'd earlier had some assistance in handling the burial formalities for Vlad Holt's ashes.

The café was dark inside, with lamps lit on the tables, and a shade crossed Hoffmann's face and chopped off one corner of the tablecloth in gold on white, like random window light on the snow.

Hoffmann had a white face, bloated like the spring snows, but now it looked frozen, as if it'd never really melted. He'd been different the other time, but I could hardly remember him ever smiling. His lips were bloodless and somewhat crumpled, and his eyes were dark, looking almost black in the lamp light, deep and immobile under his pendent eyelids and his thick, low, pale eyebrows. He was a blonde man, totally gray now, with thinned hair on his forehead and a strong, slightly plumped body under the pullover. We hardly made our way to his table before he stood up, leaving a tip, and put on his parka.

"You'll go live at my place, for the moment," Hoffmann said. "That's the most peaceful place in whole Berlin." He ran his eyes across our faces, as if reading our question, then replied, "There can be official and non-official relations. For the spoilt official relations, one may bring and accept apologies; but no apologies are accepted for spoilt off-the-record matters."

"Thank you," Vlad nodded.

Who was this Ernest Hoffmann? We considered him a retired counterintelligence officer. At least, we could read the years of service at a low salary on his face without much effort.

This trial against Schumann appeared at the intersection of several secret services, and each and every step in this action was subject to approval of the German counterintelligence. But Vlad and I had not seen anyone else so far. There must have been something underway all this time, kind of behind closed doors. All we could do was guess. It was actually for the better that Hoffmann had stepped in; otherwise I would have considered all this nonsense to be a mere fantasy of Vlad's. I'd met Hoffmann at the cemetery and he'd taken me under my arm. At that point, I'd wanted to ask him something in a polite way but realized there were no questions to ask, and nothing to answer; that he was aware of everything and I could feel that surprising serenity about him. He came in imperceptibly and left so easily, without saying goodbye, without many words, as if telling us that he would be back. He'd said that I could drop in any time for a cup of coffee. He probably wished to believe it, but he was hardly able to protect Vlad. And then, why would he do it?

Somewhere midway to Potsdam, Hoffmann turned onto a narrow road. His Opel's wheels crushed the ice crust along the narrow street. Hoffmann had a small, pretty, old half-timber house, with freshly whitewashed walls, behind the front garden, filled with snow that blared with its sparkling whiteness. A narrow path cleaned from the snow lead to the house, its porch with the wild grape covered in snow. The windows looked dim, steamed up inside, their lower edges patterned in frost flowers.

"Here, this is a minor Fort Knox. It maybe requires some cleaning. So, be my guests," he said, opening the door to the chilly rooms with their whitewashed walls and dark old furniture. "It will soon get warmer in here. You may light the fireplace for the time being."

As Hoffman tried to light a fire in the fireplace, he sometimes cast a look at Vlad, to either evaluate him or find out whether he could understand him properly. I was busy making coffee and sandwiches. After exchanging looks with Hofmann, I thought he was talking the same language as Vlad. As for me, he found me rather a nuisance.

"The prosecution had a witness, Ivan, and now he's gone. He was that very Smith who used to live in Berlin under your own name, and then under the name of Holt. You must have wanted to act as him when you came to the US Embassy and signed your confession statement. How much did they pay you, Leman, for signing that confession paper?" he asked Vlad.

"Two hundred thousand."

"That's not bad. What were you thinking?"

"My mother."

"Do you intend on acting as an agent in court?" Hoffman asked him, already knowing the answer.

"They told me it was to ruin the court case. It was not so hard to find out who I really was. I was referred to a lawyer and they told me to rush to him, so he could handle the whole thing with the court. Ernest, you should understand: otherwise they would have found me, and I would have successfully become the dead body of that damn Smith. I've seen the man before. We do look very similar."

"Yes, that was pretty clear," Hoffman unwillingly nodded. "You're rather smart, Leman. And then, you're lucky. This Ivan has turned out to be handy; he told them everything they must have wanted to hear from him. But then, you know, something is still missing. You are supposed to say this, instead of him."

"How do I do it? I'm no actor." Vlad unwillingly started back.

"No-no. You've got to tell them that one day you happened to come across this Smith, just as you found out about him holding your passport. Later on, you've kind of been looking after him; and not just on one occasion. Otherwise, why would you both have one and the same passport of Vlad Holt, right? So you sort of know a bit more about him than you say. Or, it looks like you may know something about him. That's what you'll tell them. It will be nothing more than a conversation at the lawyer's office. It's not for the court; you are not a witness, really."

Vlad looked up from the window and followed, with his eyes, a tall young man in a track jacket, walking with his shepherd dog. He asked,

"Shall I give you a call, or come up to that guy over there?" and he nodded in the window's direction.

"Give me a call. He's supposed to gun you down in case you walk out anywhere," Hoffmann snorted.

Hoffman spoke noncommittally, but still it was pretty clear what the thing was about. He said that he had a few clients who wished to get Leman because it was clear that Leman knew about Ivan somewhat more than one could from first sight, and in fact, they were ready to take up Leman even under the guise of Ivan. There were other people who preferred not to give away Leman for the same, other reason. And the third party was ready to give away Leman to anyone, and in whatever way, as they could see no one else in him but Leman; a man who so much resembled Ivan. Ivan was nowhere to be found, and Leman was not trying to escape – that is, why not do so? One could not give it a better wording.

That is why there was a general wish for Leman to tell everything he knew about Ivan, at the lawyer's office.

Hoffmann said,

"Of course, you may not really know this. At the moment, this is of no matter to anyone. That's a wish you'll have to fulfill. That's it."

"And what happens after I do it?" Vlad asked him.

"Then you'll have your face slightly changed, you'll be issued some new paperwork, and then you'll finally get your own fingerprints, with which you won't be ever handled by anyone any more. As per this new paperwork, you'll be a bank robber. In exchange, we'll make them promise that Smith, whoever he truly is, and everything else in connection with him, including the people he may have known, will never again have to be a witness, and will not be considered as a source in future." Running his eyes once again across Vlad's face, Hoffmann added, "That's a good enough proposal."

"You don't have to explain all these things to me, Ernest. I'm familiar with the sound of empty promises," Vlad interrupted him.

"As you wish. You'll have to refuse the name of Andreas Leman. Due to this resemblance, someone may still wish to obtain Ivan. 'Till now, we don't really know where he may be and what he may be doing... That sonofabitch may still have time enough to make up something."

"Do I have to leave my fingerprints?" Vlad asked.

"You've already left some. I took them last time, when visiting your place, and checked them on the database. There is a partial match with the guy who robbed a bank at age seventeen. His family had to move to Dusseldorf, and then he quickly disappeared. So you'll make a hundred percent German. You'll be given his identity documents. That's it."

"Why is this partial match?" Vlad wondered.

"He got his fingers burnt. I guess he must have wanted to make the same kind of career as her compatriot, Alvin Karpis," Hoffmann replied, with a nod in my direction.

"I need to know exactly what I have to say."

"Oh, that's no big secret," Hoffmann answered with ease. "The whole story is so outdated by now, so... You'll have to reconfirm just one fact. The man able to reconfirm the same has fallen asleep at the wheel, knocked up against a MAN truck."

"Oh, that's an inspirational overture," Vlad nodded. "Has the man got a name?"

"Yes. This information is kept confidential. His name can be told only in presence of a damn lot of people. If someone comes to understand that you are the only person who knows this name, I'm afraid it may harm you. That's why that guy is walking his shepherd dog out there. For you, this name is nothing but a name. You must have heard it incidentally when tracking Smith, the man living under your name. Is that clear? Another person able to reconfirm the same, Ivan, has proven to be really good as Smith; but he is there no more."

Hoffman said that Ivan had been working with the Russian companies involved in the buyup of their foreign debt in the free market, as it was scattered, at that time, in different private hands, in bills. The total amount of the Russian debt was known; this debt was officially recognized. It was important to confirm that twenty years ago, the repayment of the four billion dollar debt had been rescheduled. And further on, it seemed enough to say about talks carried out in connection with this debt being rescheduled and then partially written off in exchange for the Russian side's promise not to provide any assistance to... Hoffmann stopped talking for a moment, and then remarked that it was to be phrased in a somewhat more delicate way. Russia was supposed to convince that particular politician to leave his post quietly. Then, after a glance at Vlad, he told him,

"Roughly speaking, in exchange for this debt, someone was sold. That was that man's price."

"Miloševic," Vlad nodded. "It sounds more like delirium from the mental clinic than an actual fact. Wait. There must have been talks... But no one can really confirm the fact of those talks ever taking place, as all the evidence was with the man who's fallen asleep at his wheel."

"Exactly so. Yet, the debt in question has been rescheduled and finally written off. That's a fact. You are only supposed to reconfirm this particular fact and some conversations around it. All these conversations seem rather truthful, as you could actually name the person who must have known about them. Ivan would be able to tell us more precisely, as all those bills used to be bought up by several companies in San Francisco and, surely, the debt rescheduling or write off could not have gone unnoticed; there must have been plenty of talks about it. I don't know how you put it. You may give the name, or something, to make them understand that you've got what they meant, there. A hint is enough. Could you invent something?"

"Fuck it all. Ernest, what can I possibly know of the damn bills of some fucking country?" Vlad started saying, and stopped under that glance of his, then asking, "That's not all, isn't it?"

"Then, again, a similar rescheduling has taken place just recently. It's been in the newspapers. You can tell them that once you read it in the newspaper, about another part of this debt getting reduced in size, in a similar way, then all of a sudden... There's been a hell of a lot written about this... so you may have just thought that it was the price of yet another person..."

"Which one?"

"There is a war over there. It's not so hard to figure out. You may actually do without giving his name; it can be just a guess of yours — that'll be enough. You can't really play the fool, Leman; you've got some offshore companies, you know oats in the accounts, and you've got an idea of what money laundering means. Do you think they haven't found out as much?" Hoffmann screwed up his face. "That's not a trial. They won't expose you in court. I cannot really promise this, but I'll do my best to see that it never happens."

"Ernest, I'm sorry, I've got a silly question. That agent Smith, as I understand, was eventually found. It turned out to be Ivan. He told them he was Smith. So this Ivan: was he truly Smith, or could there have been someone else?"

Hoffmann looked at Vlad point-blank, as if seeing him for the first time.

"Leman, are you ready to be a Russian agent again? And would you like to sign yet another confession statement?" he asked him, and froze for a split second, as if going back to some other thoughts of his. "Have you smoked too much pot? Or has she told you that you're a real smart agent in bed? Do you understand what you've stepped into? Do you know what you've pulled her into? Do you know how much I'm sick and tired of you? Remember, your name has been exploited by a person that in some fucking way is linked to the Russian intelligence. You've put your foot into this crap along with him, for the misfortune of this resemblance to him. Is that clear?"

"Ernest, I'm sorry. I was just kidding."

"The fuck with your kidding. Would you kindly take some time and think of where you could have heard that conversation about Smith? And now the main thing, Leman. Someone paid you for that visit of yours to the US Embassy, and for writing that confession statement of you being Smith. Who paid you? Can you recollect that person? Would you be able to provide a description of him?"

"Yes," Vlad nodded.

"Think about it. I'll drop in tomorrow and we'll talk; then you'll tell about it at the lawyer's office, I'll hand you the new documents, and then, hopefully, we won't see each other again."

"Ernest, who the hell needs that fucking fact?"

"Some newspaper editor. He doesn't really want to publish an article without a proper source. Even if it's bullshit, and not really worth a thing. I guess the man was just scared by someone."

"Ernest, who would be able to confirm what I'll say?"

"If all things match, there is one more person who can reconfirm it. I have no idea who it can be."

Vlad said that he would need to log on the internet; but, of course, he would not send or receive anything.

"You may use my computer," Hoffmann said, showing him the back room. "There is a bedroom. In the fridge, you will find some cold chicken and vodka. You should not go out. Is that clear?"

"Ernest... Why is all this happening? Tell me honestly."

"To my mind, Ivan has been introduced to this game for other reasons that have nothing to do with the prosecution of Schumann. I'm not the only person to think so. I guess there must be a valid cause. They say that you should tell all this, so that Ivan can't go too far. He's forgotten to say goodbye. Could he send us a postcard for Christmas, maybe? Well, I don't really share this point, so there must be something else. So, the person who's fallen asleep at his wheel; his name was Philippe Amsel."

Ernest closed the door and winced, either from the snow thrown by the wind right into his face or recollecting his recent conversation with Nick. He was not so quick to understand what Nick had been talking about.

"Look, this Leman looks rather like a retail drug dealer. What the fuck could he know of all those damn bills of some distant country he would be hardly able to find on the map?!"

"Ivan would be able to tell this, but he looks so much like Amsel. He could be Amsel. Even if he is not actually Amsel, he seems the best Amsel we can get. But I've lost him now."

"Four billion? Foreign debt? Even a banker would not be able to figure it out so quickly. Although... Leman has been involved in money laundering, in effect, he is an accountant. He might figure out. Oh gosh, I just pictured his face, the kind he may have, if I tell him about these four billion. Why do you need this Amsel?"

"The mole must have been aware of those negotiations and informed of who this Amsel was. That should make the mole nervous."

"Hmm, it's like the military base, over here," Vlad snorted after having a look around a cramped room under a low ceiling with dark beam ribs, once the door closed behind Hoffmann.

"We're trapped. We can't really run away, and there is nowhere to go."

"Erm, I actually feel better here." Vlad brushed it aside. "Hmm, look, this must be the reason why I'm still alive."

"Vlad, why have you guessed what Hoffman wanted to hear from you? Oh god, it was like... as if he was checking you out. Why did you know what to tell him, there?"

"I did not really know. He let me read it on his face. It's good to play poker with him. Shit, I thought I might goof up."

"What will you say about the person who paid you for writing that confession statement at the embassy?"

"No idea."

"What do you mean by "official" and "nonofficial" relations? What was Hoffmann talking about?" I wondered.

"Hoffmann, I guess, is not just a retired counterintelligence man. He must have some weight in this world. He still maintains his relationship with other secret services; with the Russian side for sure –

the kind of relations no one is interested in spoiling. It's just silly to lose that kind of contact."

"How do you find it by turning into a bank robber?" I intended to smile.

"I've been dreaming of robbing a bank all my life. How does it usually happen?" Vlad inquired.

"Do you mean the raiders? Victor has been telling me. He said that one day he came to the bank and they still found it hard to believe in their bank seizure. They tried to resist. The female secretaries withdrew from Victor, the bank staff did their best not to come into view, and there were plenty of half-open doors, scared looks, and paperwork scattered around the floor... He said that, having a look around, he thought, *Here, this bank is mine.*"

"That's nice."

"Vlad, so what about that second man who was possibly sold for the partial remission of the foreign debt? Who can it be?" I wondered.

"Gaddafi. Russia will not offer any help to Libya. There is one simple reason – it's actually one and the same thing. Russia cannot really help it; it's powerless."

That was utter bullshit. How could one link those two absolutely unrelated facts – even more so, since that other fact had never really occurred? Or, otherwise, one could speak of the Russian debt remittance, but it could have happened for any other reason. There was only logic which hinted that if something had happened once, it might well happen again. Vlad said that this particular style – that is, setting links between two absolutely unrelated events – was a common trait of the British Intelligence's work. But if viewed from a different angle, through the eyes of the person who would be reading the newspaper article, it would rather look like a political conspiracy; just the kind the Americans loved, with its big money and the sale of two presidents for debt relief...

"Hollywood may relax," Vlad shrugged.

"Have all of them gone crazy? This is not politics. It's liquid manure, in which all of the politicians have bathed."

"Don't even think about it; it's a thing of the past. No one really wants it here. That's simply some kind of a fucking scenario. And who the hell might have written it? What sick mind could this great idea have come to?"

"Vlad, this is all fine for the yellow press; nothing more. One can't really get stars on his shoulder straps for this kind of job."

"What is this? Who is getting fucked over? I feel like an idiot."

Even a banker would not be able to work it out so easily... Driving his car out of the narrow lanes, Ernest seemed to hear his own voice echo. *Even a banker would not be able to work it out... Even a banker...*

He brought his car to a halt at the railway station, came up to a pay phone, then dialed Schumann's number and told him,

"You should brush the hell off any trace of your transactions with the French banks," and he cut off.

CHAPTER FOUR

IT'S NOT WHAT YOU THINK

We stopped talking. Why was there such a high price set for that kind of supposition, such as this arrangement between several secret services so that the States would not insist on Ivan's delivery? What could the Russians possibly lose, on this? Nothing, really. No one would ever believe in this bullshit. True, the talks could have possibly taken place; but had they *really* taken place? It was a matter of twenty years ago. In what way could Russia have helped Yugoslavia? No way. I found it hard to think about it, but Russia was rather weak and powerless at that time, as well as now; this was too evident. Vlad advised me to stop thinking about such things, as the story they wished to hear from Vlad at this point really had nothing to do with reality. It was more like talking in a mental clinic.

"I feel bad. I've got to drink something," I said, and went to have some vodka.

"Could you pour me some, too?" Vlad requested.

He seemed to be thinking of something else. He gave a sigh of relief, as he must have feared they would ask him to give the name of someone to whom it could cost their life, or quite a few years in prison. This is what Vlad must have feared most of all. He probably feared that he would not be able to tell it. He must have been thinking about it from the very beginning, as soon as they'd burnt him up. All this time he must have imagined himself in court, naming someone he knew nothing about... It seemed, indeed, so scary.

And this... this seemed no big deal. This particular person, Philippe Amsel, appeared to be long dead. It was about a newspaper article, nothing else. It was about the admission of the fact that Russia could not really join the war in Libya, and one of the possible reasons given by some kind of analyst... Russia would, anyway, restrain from joining that war, whatever the true reason was. Surely

Russia would send some hired men there; but it was still not quite the same thing.

I did not know what to think, now. I actually wished to enjoy the thought of us being safe in here, for a while, rather than hanging around the city by night or sitting in a cage. In here we had a warm bed, as the rooms were well heated, now. This place was rather cozy. I made myself tea with honey and eagerly took a bite of sandwich.

Vlad reached for a cup of tea and a sandwich, and then jerked back his fingers, as if they'd gotten burned, so they froze, crooked in the air.

"There must be something fishy in there," Vlad said. "I have no wish to tell this. Ivan's choice was not to tell this. He must have had a good reason. What could the reason be?"

"Vlad, it should not do any harm to anyone, really... That would be an assumption of yours; something that was repeated later on by a journalist. It's going to be no more than press gossip. And the journalist requires a valid source. That's it. As for you: on the contrary, you have chances to play the dead body of Ivan. It would not really come to anyone's mind that you are now about to determine the fate of the President. At the moment, we've got to think how you might have learnt about it or heard it from Ivan, while he was living under the name of Leman."

"Of course, it's not the thing. I'm supposed to resolve a minor task only. What it be? What's the damn task?! Where is it? I cannot see through it. Fine... I can see it now."

Vlad clicked his lighter nervously, and then he started smoking, went to the window, opened the window sash a crack, and expelled smoke into the icy air, transparent plumes flowing out of the window.

"Could you pour me more vodka, please?" he requested, his voice somewhat changed. "For a start, let's say that Ivan was Smith, a witness against the banker Schumann. A witness is a witness, no matter if it's for the court or a mere conversation. I have never taken it the wrong way, as to why they may need this Smith. I've known it all this time. I'll give the name of that person, and as soon as I name him, the man will be finished. Can you see someone else in there, except this banker Schumann? I can't. Then, this person must be the banker Schumann."

"Hoffmann has not told us this. He would have warned us, if he'd known this. Could he have remained unaware of it? No, Vlad; Hoffmann could not really keep it from us. Or could he have not known, really?" The guess flashed through my mind as I glanced at Vlad's face.

"It's either that he's unaware or otherwise... Maybe Hoffmann has not told us because I'm not supposed to know this?"

"Do you think all these politics may be in connection with Schumann? And how?!" I could not figure out any link, and I did not really want to suspect Hoffmann.

"There must be some connection. The American side intends to break Schumann. It's probably next to impossible to resist their wish. So the Germans give away Schumann. That's a fact already. This is how I read it on Hoffmann's face."

"Does that mean that Ivan had a good reason to flee? He did not want to tell this. It turns out it's not just press gossip..."

"It may kill Schumann." Vlad said this with confidence, after having a drink of vodka, and then started smoking again.

"But how?"

This man, Philippe Amsel... he is somehow connected with Schumann. But how? He died. He was deemed dead. If he suddenly appears alive, it will mean that new negotiations are going on, and all the old shit will come out. That's where the "old bomb" in Langley is laid. A living bomb. This is this man, Philippe Amsel. He has to say something. He should say something about Schumann.

Berlin, Hoffmann's office, February 2011

For Nick it was not so hard to set a rumor about the Agency that during these twenty years Moscow had been keeping the copies of the CIA paperwork regarding the negotiations. It was much more complicated to link this paperwork to Schumann.

Nick managed to find out that the Russian group spymaster was about to be out of the Russian prison, the man who'd earlier lived in San Francisco under the name Dan Wald. Nick came to learn that Dan Wald was about to be out of jail with his name Philippe Amsel. And he'd been the person in charge of the negotiations regarding the foreign debt remittance. For everyone he'd died twenty years ago in a road accident. It was probably a convenient solution for all parties. And now he was about to emerge from jail, grown old and castaway. And even if the Russian group he used to head was nowhere to be found, one could still give the appearance that this group used to exist before.

Several years ago the last members of this group had been arrested. Had they been real agents? No, definitely they had not. It was obvious to Nick, as distinct from others, who could only see in these people what they wanted to see. In fact, all three of these men arrested on suspicion of espionage used to know each other and sometimes meet, so people had seen them together. Not a single Russian deep cover agent was supposed to know another one, it was a strict rule prescribed by Moscow. They could sometimes work in pairs, but they never met with any other sleepers. So these guys must have been dummies.

For Nick it did not really matter. For him it was important that these men could give the appearance of a Russian group, and Schumann was supposed to come before the court as one of the group members from San Francisco.

Dan Wald had supplied the list of the agents expected to be recruited by the Russian secret services within the CIA. And the man probably remembered to whom he'd handed this list and could name Todd Miller, so Miller would be done with.

Nick only thought so. It was just an idea of his. And he turned it over in his mind, in different ways. Nick never thought of the possibility to face this Wald, and he did not expect to ask the man this question regarding that list. He pictured him as a run-down old man who must have lost his memory... It did not matter! For this project of his he did not really need any face-to-face contact. It seemed enough to announce that Dan Wald turned up and his name was Philippe Amsel.

Potsdam, Monday 21st, about 12 p.m.

"Schumann will crash down," I said, still in disbelief that this outcome was possible.

But then, why not? I could suddenly see it from a different angle. I could see the lawyer's white shirts, like melting ice carried away through the dim waters, and Vlad in office, and all those lawyers, the sparkling tables showing the reflections of the men. He looked too much similar to Ivan. This is what was supposed to be seen in him. Nothing else was required from Vlad. It did not really matter what Vlad would say. They just wanted this resemblance. Vlad would take Ivan's seat, his face would be reflected in the glass doors, and he'd be observed by all those people who'd earlier seen Ivan from behind those same doors – by a damn lot of people. Through the glass and from close-up, they would all see Vlad as Ivan.

Otherwise, why would they need this Leman; someone to reconfirm the words of a runaway witness? It was like a catch-up confirmation. It might all look like Ivan saying it himself, with the seat still warm from his behind in the same conference room, where he had spoken of San Francisco and the Russian group, and about the companies involved in the buyup of foreign debt bills, discreetly, at a good price. These words of Leman would, rather, echo Ivan's words. The men were truly copies of each other. It was difficult to tell them one from another. A week or two would pass, and even the lawyers would forget which of them had really spoken of the foreign debt rescheduling. These were mere generalizations. Such words could come from just about anyone. It seemed a mere talk of far too much big money; of far too many big-scale politics: a mere conversation. Leman could have overheard Ivan talking to someone about it. He could have heard this figure of four billion. It was such a big amount that he must have remembered it; it not just a gambling debt.

Time would do its job, so the faces of Ivan and Leman would merge into one and all this bullshit would assume the same kind of significance and would convince staff, just like everything else that Ivan had told them. Ivan had delivered a long speech. From all he'd told them, it was only clear that he used to be agent Smith, working in San Francisco. Would anyone ever listen to the record? No, surely not. It would all look as if Ivan had already told something, and that Leman, a common business person and a petty drug dealer, an involuntary back-up copy of the Russian agent involved in this buyup of the foreign debt bills, had only reconfirmed the agent's words. In fact, who of these two men was supposed to speak of the debt remittance? What a drug dealer could ever know of how the open market of foreign debts really worked? Only Ivan knew this. This was obvious.

"Yes, the banker is not the kind of man to whom you may issue another set of identity documents and then kick him out to have a rest somewhere far away. Schumann would not go for it. They really wish to finish him off," Vlad said, starting to smoke.

CHAPTER FIVE

THE LIVING BOMB

"This is a multi-move scheme," Vlad cussed. "I'm not much fond of multi-move schemes. I did not think the Americans would play it this way... it's not their favorite scheme, actually; not their style. No – actually, it's a British scheme set up by a British guy, tailor-made for the American side. That means there must be a British analyst working for the Americans. It's a pity I will never know who that bastard is ."

"Wait a bit, Vlad; do you think that's the work of a single man? As I understand it from your own words, this Schumann must have become an operation that the Americans now wish to bring to a logical end. And a dead Schumann is not what they need. It must be something like that."

"Until now, I was thinking the same thing. But then, it looks like there is a person who knows about Schumann more than others, and he probably knows more about those talks than all those other people. The scheme must have come from him... And they must have given credence to his opinion. This man is related to the British Intelligence, right? What the hell is this?"

"Is it about a single person?"

"True, um, as this Schumann seems a very close and clear target. If it were the British Intelligence, their goal would be more of a high-scale and a longer throw, and there would be many more of those moves. The British would not really link these two cases of debt remittance so clearly. They would do it in a more subtle way, and this is rough work. The British usually cover similar things another way, by creating distractions, and then they work in a more delicate fashion. But in this story there is no coverage, which means that the Americans must have done it in haste, probably naming it Version Two of Schumann's Execution. Then number three will follow, and so on and so forth, until Schumann dies of heart failure right in the courtroom."

Vlad gave this some thought. He started to smoke, blowing the smoke into the half-open window, then finally uttered,

"The fucking worst thing about this story is that it could be true."

I froze on the spot. Somewhere in the depth of the rooms I could hear the clock clearly tick, as if in an empty space. It seemed to have ticked off the time of some other dimension. I had a feeling that all of it was happening, but not to me.

"Vlad, can it be true, really? How come? They have to agree on such things with the president. I can't believe it..."

"It's not the thing." Vlad stared into the window unseeingly, frozen to the spot.

"So what is it, then?"

"Look. There've been some negotiations. The man who used to know about it has fallen asleep at his wheel and died. Or otherwise, they may have arranged for this road accident. Some paperwork still remains, which has been peacefully kept in Langley's archives for twenty years. Then a Russian turncoat steps in and says that this paperwork has been copied, and the copies must be held somewhere in Lubyanka – that's if the KGB's finance department was in charge of the same. That means there must have been a mole in Langley for over twenty years. This is about a living bomb set some twenty years ago, that has exploded just now."

"Hmm... and these documents contain the names of the companies in San Francisco and New York, by means of which the foreign debt bills must have been getting bought up. That is why they must have started looking for that Russian group."

"Looks like it."

"Where could this whole story have come from? Who asked this turncoat to delve through that old paperwork?"

"I guess they must have requested not quite those documents, but everything in connection with the fourteenth department of KGB. He must have brought them these documents along with some other paperwork. And there it must have exploded, really."

"Does that mean that Ivan has been providing the cover-up for that mole; for the man sitting somewhere in Langley for twenty years?"

"Yes. And there must have been more than a single mole. I've been thinking about it. Let us assume there are two moles in there. One is on the verge of exposure and is ready to flee. And they find him through a witness in Berlin, Smith, who happened to disclose him just by chance. In a nutshell: the man is constrained to escape. But would he really be able to do it? Who knows? So the second mole, a real one, who is someone of higher value and more discreet, may sigh with relief. That other man is still warm in his office. There must be complete checkups underway. They might discover that second mole accidentally. To prevent it, Ivan steps in and tells the name of the first mole. So this mole escapes at the right point and thus takes on all those failures that must have been due to both of them. Everything would get written off to just one mole. The second one would peacefully continue his work. It appears the best possible cover. No one has to die. The mole is known. In fact, it's always good to pin things on someone who is dead, but in this situation they can't really have just a mere dead man. Ivan probably worried about the mole. It's because of this mole that Ivan had to come up, eventually. It must have been the true reason why he chose to act as a witness in court. It's been the same earlier, and the same will work in future, since the world is made this way – and not just the spy world. If someone really wants to get something, he is usually given what he wants. The Americans wish to get a Russian mole – so they will get a Russian mole."

"You actually say it the way Victor used to put things, that other time... It's actually scary. I do feel scared, Vlad."

Last time, Victor had returned to Berlin, confident that he would be able to gain everything back – with his former seat on the bank board and his spouse. But the new board had only wanted a dead man. Victor would have made an ideal dead man, as he used to be a Russian agent in the bank. So the board had eventually gained a dead Russian agent – Victor's wife.

Victor had told me, then, *They've been looking for a Russian insider, and they've got him fine. They wanted this person dead...*

"I'm really scared," Vlad echoed.

"Vlad... it's not at all about a newspaper article. You would actually have nothing to do with Schumann. As to the press, Ivan's words should have been enough, since they may be his private opinion, as he is a person who could have known."

"It must have been not enough. This Schumann probably had a really good defense. They should be able shake the money out of the newspaper for the fact that Ivan has never really told anything like that."

"This means that the defense may insist said he didn't say these words, and they would try to find out..."

"They would not really need the words, if there is proper paperwork. Still, there is supposed to be a valid witness for the paperwork. It could be an incidental witness; someone like me."

Could this Schumann have more to do with the matter than we thought? What could that dead turncoat have said; the one who was supposed to play witness against Schumann? To a greater or lesser degree, Schumann must have been related to those negotiations.

I was still unable to understand anything in there. As it turned out, the negotiations regarding that foreign debt payment rescheduling appeared all of a sudden to be the key point. It was no longer so important whether

Schumann had been recruited or not. No one would really turn back to it, once this Schumann was out of court. They would not really bring Schumann to court for a second time, with espionage charges. They probably were about to arrange some other kind of charges against him. And they probably built it on a newspaper hoax regarding the debt remittance. Thus, the prosecution could not really shift away from this Russian group, or from the witness named Smith.

Vlad started grumbling that all this bullshit looked like an assignment where the agent was supposed to kill about a dozen people with only a single bullet – just Smith.

"Let us have a look at what kind of person has died. Could he have died accidentally? Or could his death have been an outcome of those negotiations?"

I opened up my laptop to see the news. We could not risk searching for this name on the Internet.

Philippe Amsel had died in a road accident in Moscow. Further on, there were only a couple of notes: it had been his second road accident. The first one, in which Amsel had survived, was said to have taken place a week earlier.

"There've been two road accidents, one after another. What the shit. It's actually worse than a piece of shit," Vlad said in irritation, starting to smoke again.

"In what way?"

Vlad told me that in order to kill someone in a road accident, they had, first of all, to make a proper estimate: at least eight vehicles were required for this purpose. This meant there must have been eight different contractors. Then, another few people were to track him down and find out about his route. There should have been also some middlemen linking the client and the contractors. All in all, there must have been too many people aware of this attempt against Philippe Amsel. And with two road accidents, even more people must have been informed. Why wouldn't they kill him in a more primitive way? The fewer middlemen involved, the less the chance of any leaks.

"But could they have intended a road accident that looked more like a murder? For what purpose? To whom would they need to pass on the information that Amsel's death was from someone's order? Could it have been a stroke against the client? Hmm... or could they have wished to inform as many people as possible of Amsel's death?

"We would not ever know this."

"Oh, shit! I've got it! That's the thing!" Vlad shifted his still-frozen glance from the window to me, as though looking through his own thoughts. "I actually know who this Englishman is who works for the American side against Schumann."

"Who?"

"He is not an Englishman, but the same dead defector, Nathan Blatt. Do you remember? When I was burnt up, I thought that he might testify against me, and then he died. That's him. He's alive."

"How do you know?"

"If there is no one else you can think of, then he must be the man. It looks too much like him," Vlad replied evasively.

Berlin, Hoffmann's office, February 2011

Nick questioned the workability of his own plan to pull out of nonbeing and olden paperwork the ghosts of the people who, once they got fully satiated with the vibrant fear of his colleagues from the Agency, could potentially kill two living humans, that is, Schumann and that undetected

Russian mole whose name this Schumann had refused to sell.

Nick had no facts really. He had nothing but the words of Nathan Blatt, a Russian turncoat who was reported as dead. The man stayed in a cheap motel in Bronx.

Blatt, a distrustful, dull and worrisome but undemanding man, who'd once taken a quick look at the paperwork on the Russian resident's table in the Embassy, could not really raze it from his mind. He'd made some copies and paid a visit to the house of someone who'd let him understand that he did not mind receiving more information from him. It had been impossible for Blatt to come back and continue doing his work discreetly as a proper mole. The paperwork had been of too high value, probably worth billions of dollars, so the leak would have been far too obvious.

He'd come to play a computer game with the man's kids, waiting for him to come home. This agent determined to recruit Blatt had immediately guessed what was on his mind when seeing Blatt in his own house. After five minutes a financial analyst had arrived, and it had taken him only two minutes to make sense of the paperwork, he'd nodded and left. Blatt had given a sigh of relief. His new life had started from that point on, a common American's life. He'd been issued a Green Card and given fifteen thousand dollars a year, and then everyone seemed to have forgotten about him. Initially he used to be in a fury, as he could not even go to a bar on that little money, not to speak of inviting a woman to his place, but with time his life somehow resumed its natural course. Nick had joined the Agency when Blatt, plain forgotten by everyone, turned an honest penny by providing consultancy in a private security firm.

One day, when reviewing some old reports received from a Russian source of MI-6, it had come to Nick's mind that the Russians could not have been aware of this; they must have been given a hint by someone inside the CIA. The reports appeared to be quite old, so Nick had retrieved a few other old reports and then announced his intention to work with Blatt.

Blatt, among other things, had taken some training in a so called "British school" in Moscow. For a week he'd been in the same group with a deep cover agent who'd either lived a very long time in the United States or was a son of Russian aliens, a blonde man with a hardly visible scar under his chin. When shown the picture of the visitor to the US Embassy in Berlin delivering a confession of him being Harvey Smith, Blatt had told Nick,

"We could reanimate Amsel so he kills Schumann."

Amsel had resurrected and murdered Blatt.

CHAPTER SIX

NOT THE ONE YOU THINK

Tuesday 22nd, around 10.00 a.m.

"Ivan preferred not to speak about it. He must have known that I would get into this fix. He should have warned me somehow," Vlad started pacing about.

"What was your communication channel? Was it through the lawyer's office?"

"Yes, one could drop in and request some case reference number, and then instead tell them my number."

"Which number?"

"Everyone has a personal number. But now that my case file resurfaced, this number of mine must be known to every man and his dog. We can still try."

Vlad thought that Ivan could still be somewhere in the country. He could also know where we lived, and might drop something there. He could have learned the telephone number of Vlad's company, through which Vlad was normally contacted by the partners in the deal; so he could give us a call.

I pushed the half-open wicker door and walked into the street. The young man with a shepherd dog waved to me in a friendly way, and coming up to me, he suggested,

"If you are heading to the food shop over there, you may find excellent sausage," he made a gesture in the direction of a small store that I could clearly see from where I stood.

"No, I'm going to Zehlendorf to pick up the discs with the press, and I will be back soon."

There were no footprints on the doorsteps of our old house. The courtyard looked as usual: clean from the snow, like the lake surface on a quiet evening. The house seemed still warm inside, and somewhat more inhabited among all those other abandoned and cold buildings cramped around this courtyard. At the entrance hall and in the house corridors I could smell the sweet odor of mildew which had still not died, out in this cold.

So many times on my way back to this apartment I thought that one day I would open the door into this warm, smoke-filled room and find out Vlad was there no more. He used to wait for me here, crooked over his laptop in the half-dark in his white T-shirt, his pale face lit with the screen light, in his narrow glasses; on the edges of which I could see dim flecks play. I would never see him again that way. At this point we no longer had this home of ours. We kept losing one thing after another, and there seemed to be no end to it.

I went upstairs and stopped at the stairwell. I could smell the cigarette smoke. What the hell? Or had Vlad smoked up a whole pack before departure? He could have done it, why not? Last time he'd said that any cigarette could turn out to be the last one for him. But no, this cigarette odor was rather recent, damn it. After giving it some thought, I realized that my steps against the brick rubble must have been heard all along the empty frost-bound corridor. I turned the key in the door lock, but the door seemed somewhat frozen, so I pulled the doorknob and the door screeched; yet it still didn't open. I could hear someone coming from inside the room, up to the door; I could hear it very well from where I stood, as if the rooms were frozen through already.

Vlad opened the door. It was a hallucination. Now I could really understand Richter. The man was not quite like Vlad, yet everything in him looked so similar: his sharp, bird-like nose, his swollen lower eyelids, his pale eyebrows and eyelashes. It was not quite the thing, but his sex appeal immediately caught my eyes so that I would not even question the resemblance.

For a split second it seemed to me that Vlad had never really left the place; that everything remained as usual. On the table there was a cup of coffee, the mini cakes, and an ashtray.

"Would you like some cake? Coffee?" he offered.

"Yeah. Hi, Ivan. Aren't you cold in here?"

"I've just come. Where are you staying now?" Ivan asked, inviting me to the kitchen, where he started making coffee.

"Ivan, look, I've told them where I'm heading to. You'd better go."

"I'll go if needed. I've come through the attic, from the back stairs."

"We are now staying as guests with a person who's offered us a bargain: new identity documents and doing away with this threat of delivery to the States, in exchange for some bullshit for a newspaper article."

"Well, I've also been approached with a similar proposal. I refused, for some personal reasons. Regrettably, I've already told them enough. I just wanted them to believe me. Andreas is in a different situation. Or do you still call him Vlad?" I nodded, and he continued. "He may still ride out, but I can't. The main point is, is Vlad aware of what he is supposed to tell? That's about the rescheduling of a foreign debt payment. Have they give you the name of the person in charge of the negotiations; the man who died later on?"

"Yes."

"I don't think that getting more information about this man could help Vlad in any way, really. It's more important for him to think of how he could possibly get out of this story. I guess this newspaper affair would hit Schumann. It can't be otherwise, now that I've played a witness against him."

"Yes, Vlad also understands it in a similar way."

"I can roughly guess who could have suggested initiating a new court process against Schumann in this particular way. Even if that's not the man, for Vlad, it would really be better to tell it *was* him. I've seen the death notice, but in fact, everything that the prosecution may find against Schumann must be coming from one and the same single source. If there are no other sources, this person must be the source. His name is Nathan Blatt. He probably knows something about Schumann; something that no one else is able to either confirm or prove. This is about his words only, but the cost may be rather high for Schumann."

"Vlad has already guessed who the man is."

"I cannot really help you to find the man. I just have no idea where they may be hiding him. It would be better to somehow cheat him, but we are pressed for time. Vlad should tell his name – in whatsoever context, but he should reveal this name. And then Blatt would no longer be the source. If Vlad could describe the man's appearance, that should be fine. He should remember him. His forehead is crossed with two wrinkles, deep and vertical. He must have seen him in Moscow."

"Where?!" I asked him in whisper, as if choking.

Vlad had been telling lies to me all this time.

"Would you like to try this mini cake? Here's coffee," Ivan said, placing a cup of coffee in front of me the way people say, *Hush, hush, now; everything is fine.* "Has Vlad never told you? He must have spent no more than two weeks over there. He must have forgotten. But he would surely be able to recollect the man. Do you have any questions?"

"No, I can ask a question of him," I retreated, thinking that whatever it was – whatever lies there might have been, and whatever way Vlad was telling me those lies – I would still trust him, to some extent.

"There is nothing I can help you with. I must be since long retired. I hope we would never see each other again. Let us have a smoke and I'll go," he suggested, lighting a cigarette for me. "I'll remain a friend."

"He knows this," I nodded.

"Vlad has no past. I've taken all of his past, along with his name, from him. It will stay with me. I will forever be Harvey Smith, whatever happens."

"He's got it all right."

"If the whole story drags on, let him start from the beginning. That is, from Schumann. Okay?"

"Fine."

"Vlad runs a business. As I get it, he buys up some debts, right?"

"That's nothing out of the ordinary. He resells these debts to some oil companies. And the latter use these debts to pay for their concessions. It's cheaper. That's it."

"Would Vlad have to get his face changed?"

"No idea." I hid my eyes behind the smoke, unwilling to tell him more.

"Do you think you would be able to replace Vlad?" His glance seemed glued to my face. I had no other option but look into his eyes.

"No, I don't think I would be able to replace Vlad. It would all be wrecked without him."

"Haven't you ever thought that one day you may get to replace me?" Ivan said while packing the coffeemaker back into its carton box.

"Don't you worry. Vlad is not that tired, yet," I replied. I had no clue what this was about.

"I mean something different. Until I have this face, I wish to keep the passport of Andreas Leman to myself. We have two identical passports, it's easy to figure out; and both were made at the same time.

Vlad… He usually factors in too many things at a time. If I hold Leman's passport, he would fear that I might also ruin that other life of his; that of Andreas Leman, the one he's been living for twenty years. He'll actually have concerns regarding that business of his. That is truly so. He would tell you that he'd rather hold me by the balls. He would decide that, since he still has Leman's passport on him, it would be a good idea to formalize your marriage. But this marriage would not be really his marriage. It would be my marriage with you, baby. Are you sure you wish to have all the joy of it?" he asked me softly.

"What's your proposal?"

"I would not really make any proposal. Life has been so shitty recently. Women have no luck with me."

"I feel ready to take risks."

"Shall we go to bed, then? I'll make us more coffee."

"There is no haste. First you get to share the money, and then the bed."

I said this by default, out of habit; it just slipped off my tongue. How could I tell this, really? That was silly. I should have kept my mouth shut. This damn good-looker was too good. Oh my god, I was such an idiot. No, that was him, really… But who would ever ask this?! That is, to hear a negative answer? Or had he never heard a *no* in his whole life? What the harlotry...

"Don't you work in futures?"

"Nope," I snapped, now realizing that Ivan probably knew enough about me; if not everything.

At least he knew that I used to be a trader, which meant he actually knew my real name. If Ivan knows who I am, then Ivan would be holding Vlad by the balls with this hand of mine. Ivan knew to play the same kind of games as Vlad did, and I did not. I could unwittingly harm Vlad. Ivan knew Vlad far too well; he could forecast all his moves. And the worst thing was: through me. Ivan would at any time be able to see Vlad just like that unknown analyst from Langley could see the British source. Vlad had once told me that it could have turned out just fine if not for that analyst in Langley, who was way too good. No matter how well MI6 covered this source, and whatever filtered information was coming from them to Langley, this person could still see it through. What the shit.

"They will be looking for me. I'm cutting off communication. It was nice to see you. I'll do my best so that we don't have to see each other again, but I can't really promise anything."

Ivan left through the door to the back stairs. I watched him go – his gait, his body shape, and his quick gestures when he rolled up his scarf. Watched him fling on his coat, pull on his hat low on his eyebrows and his dim mirrored glasses, similar to the ones Vlad had, and watched him lift his collar. No way: he wasn't Vlad.

I could see Vlad's face before my eyes, and I could hear his voice: *I don't want you to mix me up with him. Take a proper look at me ... You'll have to kill him.*

I thought in horror, *Kill him? If Ivan stayed a bit longer or could do without all those questions, I would have surely slept with him. I'm such a headless chicken. What can I do now? Shall I tell Vlad? Or could he guess it all from my face?*

Only now I could really see the point of Richter. Even with a good understanding of the situation, all the same, when looking at Ivan, I still wished to delude myself. There was something about him – something that made me trust him than I trusted my own self.

With the cold wind on my way back, I somewhat cooled down and started thinking about something else. *Oh shit, Vlad – son of a bitch, he's been telling lies to me all this time.*

What the hell had he been doing in Moscow? He'd told me all his links had been cut off. He'd been telling me that such things happened; the links could be cut off with the agent who was able to recruit someone of really high value. This person was Richter.

But I still went to buy him mini cakes. As to Ivan speaking of Vlad's possible wish to formalize my marriage to Leman while he still held this passport, I decided not to discuss it at this point, unless Vlad started speaking about it himself.

"Vlad, damn you, have you been to Moscow?!" I wondered, hardly opening the door before I spoke. "Why haven't you told me this?"

"Have you seen Ivan? Where is he?"

"No idea. He just told me the same thing you've guessed already. He also thinks that Nathan Blatt is alive. He considers him to be the only source of the American side. Vlad, what the hell have you been doing in Moscow?!"

The answer was simple. Vlad must have stolen the money. It was a pretty good reason to leave forever. He could not really tell anyone about the recruiting – not even

Ivan – at that time Ivan must have been under suspicion. Ivan probably thought that, due to this circumstance, they would have to replace the whole group; but eventually the group was dissolved. And Ivan had been constrained to stay. He could not leave. He'd stayed in San Francisco under the name of Harvey Smith. That's how they had settled it. Vlad never thought it could last for so long.

"Vlad, that is – were you actually aware of Ivan having taken this name of yours?" I asked him, still clueless.

"I knew it... but I did not know he would also have my face! And it looks so similar! As to Ivan intending to live with this face of mine, how could I know this? I did not know that he got Leman's passport, and then Holt's passport. There was information about him being in court on espionage charges. I thought he was in prison or had maybe died by now. I did not really expect to see him, as the last time I saw Ivan was twenty years ago."

When Ivan started living under the name of Smith, it was for Ivan that the Russian intelligence had provided coverage with two back-up men; one of which was that office manager Holt, the man living in New York with his three children. Later on, as the British Service had incidentally come across Vlad Holt, they'd supported this version. In Leman everyone had recognized yet another duplicate; nothing more. However, Hoffman could have guessed something. But he hardly shared that guess of his with anyone else. Vlad had much hope about this.

How long ago had this Ivan, as Smith, come to the attention of the British Service? Ivan had stepped in at such a good point. It did not look like the British had been aware of him three years ago, when they'd just started this coverup operation for Schumann. If Ivan had come up just recently, he was indeed much too good. I hope he had time enough to escape. He could not have missed the presentiment that they would wish to see him dead. As Richter had said, *This bastard is so good that everyone must have wanted to see him dead.*

Vlad had come to Moscow, handled the money, and told of his recruiting. That time, they'd sent him to join the British group for a week so that he could get to know who he was supposed to deal with. He'd been in that group together with Nathan Blatt.

Vlad had left, and after a few months he'd come to live in Berlin under the identity documents of Andreas Leman. They must have forgotten about him, as he'd thought earlier; even more so since his case file had been with the Stasi. Right now, Vlad believed that there must have been an instruction to get off his back.

The same thing must have happened this time, now that they'd burnt him up, it seemed to us. According to someone's will no one would really touch Vlad. Sure enough, this had nothing to do with Vlad, nor with the fact that they could have learned something about him, such as information that he'd truly been a Smith. This must have been due to someone of high value placed on the intelligence, it could be either one of the partners in the deal or somewhere very close, and they probably feared putting the man on his guard. There could have been more than one person of that kind. It might have been that way, for Richter. Vlad appeared to be a mere pawn in whatever game they put him into. It was rather lucky that the game went on, the way he always turned out to be the back-up for some other, more important piece.

At this point, he was supposed to be the backup for Ivan.

"I do remember everything, as if I were in Moscow just yesterday. I was on a bus, on my way from the metro station. The bus was small, it was bloody cold, and it took us an hour to leave the city. The asphalt was frozen stiff, white and covered in frost-dew. I could see the cars' white tails stretching along the highway. I remember those red berry patties. We were just six in that group; I remember every one of them. Three of these guys have become defectors. I'll find and kill him."

"Who? This Nathan Blatt?"

"Yes. There can be teachers of genius and worthless students." Vlad said this quietly, but I could see he was in rage. "Ivan was a student in the group of Kim. I've never met him alive. He used to teach people something else. You can see that Ivan is totally different. He is an idealist. Have you noticed that?"

"I had no time."

What could I have noticed at all, besides that coffeemaker, in just fifteen minutes?

"So, how do you find Ivan?" Vlad asked me, running his eyes across my face, and then said through his teeth: "I hope you know that you are a complete idiot?"

"Vlad, forgive me."

"What for? For him being better than me?"

"Vlad, I'm such a whore."

"What's Ivan's smell?"

"That's money. I could smell it from a mile away. He smells like the stock exchange on takeoff; the frosty air, the petrol, and the fresh bakery."

Only late in the evening, when we had the fireplace lit again and took seats at the table, after Vlad had eaten his third mini cake, did I finally resolve to inquire, with caution,

"Vlad, what have you been doing in Moscow? Have they been teaching you to escape the graymen? And shooting? Or did they teach you how to swallow the ampoule with poison?" I smiled, recollecting the spy movies.

"Have a better look at me, mein herz. I was only taught to jump out of bed. But I knew how to do it anyway."

CHAPTER SEVEN

THE LIVING AND THE DEAD

Wednesday 23rd, around 09.00 a.m., at the lawyer's office

Hardly opening the door, Hoffmann asked him,

"Leman, are you ready?"

"Yes."

"You've got to do what is needed."

"No problem," Vlad nodded.

"Are you sure you can tell what is required? It will be an interrogation; the kind they make for a financial expert. Besides the lawyers in front of you and a few other people, along with the editor at the far end of the conference room, behind you there will sit two more people, a financier and a finance lawyer. You would have to reply to their questions, and they would

111

let the lawyers know whether you're telling them lies or not. If they realize you are familiar with the accounts any more than a petty drug dealer, your goose is cooked."

"Don't you worry, Ernest."

Hoffmann gave us a lift up to the lawyer's office. I took a seat, waiting for Vlad in the office lobby. The conference room was spacious, just as in Ivan's case one could see a whole team and observe every gesture of his from the adjacent room. Hoffmann later told me what Vlad was telling them in there.

Vlad spoke for more than an hour. They asked him how many times and who had been giving him the money to play the role of Smith. Vlad told them he could remember that man's face to the smallest detail: he was of low stature, dried-up and wiry, around sixty, gray-haired with brown eyes, with a husky voice and no accent, a broad face with a lot of Russian in his traits, and two deep wrinkles vertically cutting across his forehead, one of which clearly longer than the other, stretching up to his hair roots.

They stopped him with the words, *This man died three months ago. When did you see him last?*

"A month or a bit more ago. He paid me two hundred thousand cash for writing the confession at the embassy, that I had truly been agent Smith."

Vlad added that he was not surprised and was ready for it, as the man was paying him not for the first time, and until this point he could easily get away with it. He also needed that money to pay back his debt for the goods. After making the payment for the goods, he became frightened, so he went to the lawyer and said he'd signed that confession for money.

Someone from those present requested the man's photo. He showed it to Vlad on his cell screen, *Is he the man?*

Vlad nodded, *That's him.* Silence fell over the room. One of the lawyers suggested,

"Let's postpone this until we get some evidence that this man is dead."

Hoffmann stood up from his seat to show Vlad a photo from his tablet computer, *Is that him?*

Vlad gave him a nod.

"There will be no such evidence. The man was alive yesterday," Hoffmann said.

The elderly man at the far end of the table finally stood up and said in a low voice, *I can only see my money lost in here,* and he left the room.

Berlin, Tuesday 22nd, around 09.00 a.m.

I was hardly in time to reach that house of ours when Hoffmann arrived. Vlad asked him to make a photo of Nathan Blatt. Hoffmann, still unable to believe what he was hearing, inquired,

"I am supposed to find a man who was staged as dead and who is now hidden in some kind of apartment or in a motel room, of which the location may be only known to a single agent; the one who was in charge of hiding him – is that so? And that's not in Berlin, but in New York. Or have I missed something here?"

"That's in New Jersey," Vlad specified.

"And what shall I start with?" Hoffmann asked again, making no secret of his annoyance, still in disbelief over what Vlad was telling him.

"You could arrange an appointment with him some place close to his apartment. It is known where he used to live, and the man was not really hiding. Could you find out his telephone number and leave a message for him?"

Vlad took the cell phone from Hoffmann's hands and gave me a nod, *Say this in Russian,* he uttered, added a few words into my ear, and then pressed the record button.

"*I failed to catch you at home, I'm waiting for you at the café next door. Kim,*" I repeated those words of his.

"Let him eventually die of heart failure," Vlad uttered in such a low voice that I could hardly hear him.

Later on I asked Vlad whether something did not really match up. Nathan Blatt was alive, and had lived a perfect, peaceful life for over twenty years. Vlad used to tell me that defectors hardly die their own deaths.

"Unless it's about refuse. This one has been long dead. That's like shooting a dead body," Vlad brushed it aside.

The Americans had since long exhausted him; it must have been at the time when he'd worked for the Russian Embassy in Washington. Such people were usually provided with a green card and assistance in employment. They stop getting paid nearly right away.

The legends grow a different kind of defector. The defectors that are born through the legend live in a different way – at least, they cannot be bought, and they are not for sale.

New Jersey, Tuesday 22nd, around 07.00 a.m.

In a motel in the Bronx, after listening to the female's voicemail at his apartment, Blatt had a quick snack, then put a recorder into his pocket and rushed out. On his way to the railway station he bought a coffee and made a call to his agent from the pay phone, telling the man he was heading for an appointment with Philippe Amsel. He was thinking about how surprising life could be at times, and of the blessings that sometimes came so handy. He'd recollected Amsel just three months ago, when realized it was a good idea to start not with Schumann but with that bank of his.

It could be no one else but him, as he was the only person not interested in Smith giving the lawyers his name – it was Amsel himself.

Wednesday 23rd, around 11.00 a.m., at the lawyer's office

"Erm, I hope no one gives a fuck about me any longer," Vlad said to Hoffmann, ready to tell him goodbye; but the latter looked away.

"Listen," Hoffmann reached for his pocket and took out the keys, "something has just happened in here. Ivan has named a person in Washington. The man used to be a Russian informant. There must have been interrogations. So could you stay for another bit, at my place?" and he handed the keys to Vlad. "I guess Ivan will now live under the name of Leman. I cannot see any other options at this point."

Vlad froze to the spot; he stared wide-eyed, as if not hearing. Clearly, something must have happened. The mole whose name Ivan had named was not able to escape. As this information about him was coming from Ivan, then... I felt unwilling to think what this could turn out to mean for Schumann and then, maybe, for Vlad as well.

Hoffmann said,

"Fortunately for you, the name of the person in charge of the talks about the debt remittance does not really matter any longer. This is insider information as of now; but I can still tell you this. The Russian informant has given the real name of the Russian group spymaster. He was Philippe Amsel."

"What else is there?" Vlad inquired automatically.

"Smith's delivery is no longer requested via official channels, they will clearly never get him alive. They wish to have him alive, since he's given the informant's name now, and he was right. He probably knows more than this. They've started hunting him. You'll be better off and safer at my place."

"Is there just one hunter?" Vlad wondered.

Ernest said that in the United States, nothing had really changed since the times of Bonnie and Clyde. Ivan would be followed by just one hireling, most probably a Russian, and he would keep searching for him until he found him.

"Thank you, Ernest," I said with gratitude, taking the keys from him with my instantly-frozen hands.

"You won't get away with a single *Thank you*. You should stay home. How do you manage walking in the street? You can't really put two words together. Where were you made?" he started grumbling.

"In the snow bank."

CHAPTER EIGHT

RUSSIAN MATRYOSHKA

Wednesday 23rd, 02.00 p.m.

"Vlad, how did you and Ivan both figure out that Blatt is alive?"

Vlad said that Blatt must have known of the Russian group, in his professional capacity, and was aware of them buying up the debts, but he was not familiar with any group members; neither the recruited agents nor the deep cover guys. If Blatt had known anyone, really, that person would have been arrested twenty years back, when Blatt had become a defector himself. Blatt was well informed of the negotiations regarding the foreign debt payment rescheduling, and he also knew who was in charge of them.

These talks could have only been handled by someone with experience in foreign debts.

Vlad used to be in the British group along with Blatt; it was an intensive course. Why had Blatt joined in? Whatever could have been the true reason? Blatt still remembered that in the same group with him there used to be an American; a blonde man, a knockout. Surely everyone in this group had a nickname, as per the rules.

"Look here." Vlad was still thinking it over. "Blatt could remember my face, and also recollected that I used to be a student in the same group with him, but who would I really be to him, in these memories? Philippe Amsel. Blatt had never known of Smith's existence. He had no idea that in court there might appear a witness Smith, until that case file of Smith's turned up on the American side. This happened at the point when I was burnt up, in mid-January."

Philippe Amsel, the way Blatt must have seen him back then, was an American citizen, which did not really matter: he could just have as well been a Russian deep cover agent all his life, living in the States. One way or another, the man was linked to the KGB's 14th Department.

Amsel was not an official, but a middleman between the American and Russian parties.

Blatt was not aware of this.

"Even I did not know that the real name of Ivan was Philippe Amsel. No one at all knows about this. Before I assumed my name of Smith, to me he used to be Dan Wald, a codename he'd lived with for a number of years," Vlad said.

There hardly remained a photo of Amsel anywhere. Blatt had probably remembered his face and realized that Amsel and Smith were one and the same person.

It might have been such that Blatt had not seen Smith in the photo right away. But once this Blatt had seen a picture of Smith, Blatt must have identified in it as the defunct Amsel. If he had been shown a photo of Leman before, he would have seen in him either Amsel, or a duplicate of him.

So what? This was nothing, really. He might have thought only that Amsel was still alive and living under the name of Smith; and later on, in Berlin, under the codename of Leman and Holt. Smith must have been a man from the Russian group under the KGB's 14th Department, for which this Amsel had been handling the talks.

So this same Smith, a living Amsel with the passport of Ivan Ivanov, had come up at the lawyer's office a few days earlier. Well, what of it, if they thought Amsel was dead? The fact of those negotiations was properly concealed.

Smith was actually better than someone newly aware of those negotiations. He really knew everything about it, as the man in charge of it. And the man was Philippe Amsel. There was no need to provide any evidence. All they needed was a qualified man able to reconfirm the fact of those negotiations; that is, Smith himself. It was enough to find a picture of Amsel, so they would have one and the same face. It could even make for a sensation. Even if that Smith was a duplicate, it did not really change anything: the resemblance was there, and that was enough.

They could take these talks for accomplished fact, then turn them into gossip, have them linked to some fact that had never taken place, and plant the seed of suspicion... This rather tricky scheme could be called "British style".

This kind of scheme could have come from Blatt; from a man well informed of the British Service's operating mode.

Blatt must have learned about Smith only as this court case against Schumann was getting ready. True, this kind of action from the American side must have taken a pretty long time. However, this witness Smith had been found by the British, be that evident or not; but it was not really like Blatt to have recollected Smith: he had never really known anyone from the Russian group. Possibly, just as Vlad had guessed earlier, Schumann had found a witness for himself of his own accord: this Smith.

Could this Blatt have been a witness against Schumann, then? It seemed as likely as not. However, Vlad had from the very beginning considered the death of Blatt to be staged for some other, more important purpose, and most probably Blatt knew something else about Schumann. He could be aware of how exactly and which particular personal data files Schumann had been buying out. In this case, it made sense to cover up for Blatt as a source and rather search for another witness.

Blatt must have started working on this scheme from the point when the case file of Smith had come into the prosecution's hands, when Michael Brown had told them of Smith being alive and operating under the name of Vlad Holt, the man in charge of the buyup of some African countries' foreign debts. For Blatt, this actually meant that Amsel was alive and busy doing his regular job.

Blatt must have seen through this witness Smith and his duplicates; all of them, in fact, serving as backups for just one person – Philippe Amsel. And it did not really change things. By that time there must have been more than enough of those backup men.

So Blatt must have started thinking of how to knock down Schumann by using the name of Amsel. This name could have been recollected only by Blatt, and then later on there must have come from the archive records all that paperwork regarding the negotiations; the copied files kept all this time in Lubyanka. This was our way of thinking. Otherwise, what would be a good explanation for this mole being detected – and from a twenty – year-old scent, incidentally?

Now that it turned out that Amsel had been the spymaster of the Russian group... And what about that photo of him? It could have hardly turned up just like that; it must have been part of his personal data, kept in Moscow. That is, only Blatt could have known how Amsel really looked. The man looked like Ivan. But this Ivan was Smith, a recruited agent who could not have been the group spymaster. The spymasters usually were Russian deep cover agents.

Ivan had refused to reply to the question regarding these negotiations, yet it had not really caused any suspicion. It was no surprise the man preferred to conceal the fact of having played the backup role for Amsel, wasn't it? This still remained to be proven. There was no time for collecting evidence; however, there was Leman, for whom it seemed enough to give the name of Amsel, so that the whole scheme could start working.

"Vlad, why haven't you told me about this Blatt earlier?" I wondered, still puzzled.

"Because he was dead! I considered killing him myself, at some point, and then I thought that Schumann must have outpaced me. It seemed so nice of him, until I realized that I would have to replace Blatt in this action against Schumann – and then I understood that it was much easier to kill me so that the British source could be properly concealed. Later on it turned out that the British had yet another dead body in stock: that is, Holt."

"Do you think this Ivan had come from the British side? Or could he have made an arrangement of sorts with the British?"

"No doubt. Still, I guess Ivan has stepped in just recently, and out of a clear blue sky, to them. No one was really prepared for a living Smith. And no one was ready for Ivan to give the name of the Russian mole. And where? In Langley? Hell knows."

Vlad said that, lucky for him, Vlad Holt's appeared corpse had appeared, and then it turned out that Smith had been covered with two different case files and some backup people, who did not really know that they were his duplicates, Holt and Leman. Leman was getting paid for visiting places, instead of Smith. And Leman owned an apartment in the name of Holt, which gave the appearance of Smith living in Berlin for a long time under the name of Holt. Fortunately, five years ago, three more people from the Russian group had been arrested. Those guys had been trained to play the role of agents; yet they were not real agents – just the backup folks. So the duplicates of Smith did not really look very special – even more so with Holt and Leman being odd men that only had some facial resemblance to Smith. However, some well trained duplicate agents might have been involved, as well.

Smith actually looked like a similar backup man, ready to substitute for the spymaster. And then, right away, it emerged that Amsel had been the spymaster for the Russian group. However, this became clear somewhat later, when Ivan disappeared.

Amsel was a good enough explanation for the appearance of all those other duplicates. One could only guess how much time it must have taken to find out why this recruited agent Smith, who was of no interest whatsoever to the Russian Intelligence, had been so thoroughly covered with backup men.

Could Smith have been aware of these negotiations in his role as a backup man? No, this was not quite up to his level.

Smith had said that he used to have a spymaster, Dan Wald; yet he'd never mentioned that they resembled each other ad nauseam.

Who could have known about the spymaster living under the name of Dan Wald until he could change his face and paperwork for that of Smith? Even if someone had known this, with a different face, Dan Wald appeared altogether a different person. So, he must have come to

Moscow as... just about anyone. The main point was that Smith and Amsel shared the same face. Or could Smith have been both Dan Wald and Amsel? It was highly improbable, with Smith being a recruited agent, which meant he was more likely to play the role of a duplicate agent. There was no one to whom we could ask this question any more, since Ivan was now gone.

Smith must have been yet another backup man within spymaster's Russian group, a deep cover agent with the codename Dan Wald who used to be in charge of the negotiations under his true name, Philippe Amsel, who then died. Or had he really died there?

What could Blatt believe, at this point? That he must have seen a duplicate, Smith? And what about Amsel? Was he really dead?

It seemed a proper Russian Matryoshka; so classic. The more you open it, the more you still think that inside the last piece there could turn up yet another little Matryoshka doll. Yet another duplicate? And then why not? This Ivan might have two different tombstones: that of Philippe Amsel in Moscow and that of Dan Wald in San Francisco.

Tuesday 22nd, around 11.00 a.m.

Philippe Amsel got off the bus at Zehlendorf and walked a few blocks along the boulevard, hiding his unshaven chin deep in his scarf and keeping his knitted cap low on his eyebrows, his face concealed behind round, dim mirrored glasses.

In his direction there came an elderly man in a dark blue duffle coat, with a bright red big check scarf showing from his open collar. The man slackened his pace, and they exchanged looks and parted.

CHAPTER NINE

THE HUNTER

Wednesday 23rd, 06.00p.m.

Vlad decided that the hunter, whoever it might be, would start searching for Ivan from Leman, so we had to be ready for the man to turn up.

"And what happens if he comes around in these parts?" I asked him, with no wish to hear the answer.

"I feel like being a honey pot," Vlad replied. "If he first comes to Hoffmann, which would be best, we would know who the man is before we actually face him here at the doorstep."

"So, shall we now wear the armor vests, here?" I intended this as a joke.

"Are you kidding? Do you think he'll be a gunman? No, mein herz, he'll be a bookkeeper. So, in case you notice a sweet old man in specs taking interest in you, that'll be him for sure."

That was an excellent conversation; the kind they have in the madhouse.

All we had to do was wait it out.

Ivan had given the name of the mole. But how could he have possibly done it? Under what pretext? What could Ivan have been talking about, as this mole's name came out? It must have been indirectly; he must have given a hint that someone in the Russian unit was aware of the Russian group's spymaster Dan Wald being an informant. And since the matter was twenty years old, they must have started looking out for the employees formerly handling that Russian group. Or could Ivan have given a more specific hint? We could not really tell what it might have been.

Eventually, the mole had given the real name of the Russian group spymaster, Philippe Amsel. From where could this mole have learned his real name?

Vlad decided that this name could have come from the Russians. The mole must have known the name of Amsel, since he was in charge of the negotiations over the debt rescheduling. And since Amsel was dead, the man was probably told that he had been the spymaster of the Russian group, without much harm to the spymaster and with some benefit for Ivan, whom they must have intended to remove from the game, thus supporting the version of him being no longer there - that he'd died, so that only Smith remained. The mole must have been intentionally misguided.

Was Amsel dead now?

But the thing was, Amsel must have seen Blatt in the British group, and Amsel knew that twenty years ago, Blatt had been informed of those negotiations. At least, by taking a proper look at the picture of Smith, this Blatt was able to eventually recognize the face of the man in charge of the negotiations – that is, the face of Amsel, mirrored in a number of his incidental copies.

Hence, this living Amsel could say that an idea to pull out and expose the negotiations of twenty years ago must have come from Blatt.

That is why Leman had said what he did about Blatt having paid him.

But who talked to Leman? Could it have been Smith? But Smith was only a backup man; he would be unaware even of his own spymaster's name – he probably knew just his codename. Smith was hardly informed of Amsel's negotiations, and Smith could not really know that Blatt had been informed about those negotiations better than anyone else.

So, Ivan must have been the cover for the spymaster, remaining a backup man till the very end, and he had never told about it. And what about the rest? He had given the name of the mole. Why? He could just as well have done without naming him. Could it have been accidental? This sometimes happened, but...

The hunter would be looking for Leman, because Leman had lied. Was Leman supposed to say who had paid him?

Schumann? Why would Schumann know about Blatt being alive? Were his tracker dogs so smart? Hardly so. The paperwork had been kept in the archives for twenty years. Blatt remembered it, and then, as it turned out, he also remembered the informant; the guy who'd worked for the Russian side. And he'd given this name of Amsel.

Bronx, Tuesday 22nd, 06.00p.m., in a motel

"That must be a trap. Except for Amsel, no one else could have guessed that I'm alive. This is no leak; he must have figured it out," Blatt told to a fattening elderly man in a dark blue duffle coat with a bright red big checked scarf and old-fashioned round glasses with a touch of light blue, behind which no one could see his eyes.

"Who is he?" the guy asked him.

"He's got a scar under his chin; he is always unshaven."

"You know what our problem is, Blatt? Your memory is much too good."

When leaving, he closed the door gently and mumbled, *I guess they would not bury you for the second time.*

Dusseldorf, Wednesday 23rd, 09.00a.m.

In the airport, a man in a dark blue duffle coat stood up from the bench beside a young man who was scrolling down his reader and drinking yogurt, and said,

"Do what you want," he paused, in which one could clearly hear *you're idiot*, "But in the morning I really need a good cup of coffee, a cigarette, and a woman."

"Don't you look at me as if I'm an idiot," the man said without looking up from his reader, as if he'd heard the word *idiot* in that pause.

"I just can't understand why the hell you need that life?" he said through his teeth, and walked away to the cafe.

He took a seat near a woman who had a cup of coffee and some croissants in front of her.

"Will you permit me to sit here? I'm also a bookkeeper; a bookkeeper under investigation. Could you offer me some coffee?"

"Anything else?" she asked him reflexively in her default tone of voice, throwing him off without looking. Then, right away, realizing that she must have been a little too quick, she looked at him with curiosity. "Why do you guess I'm a bookkeeper?"

"One cigarette, please," he pretended not to have heard her question. "That guy over there with a bottle of yogurt is supposed to carry me to Berlin. He's taken all my cash, cards, and even the keys, so that I could not escape from him. I'm really fed up with this guy. Could you give me a lift downtown?"

"And how will you handle it further on?" she wondered, b scanning his face, which was deceptively soft-looking with the apparent gloss of a wealthy life now almost gone as the smell of a branded perfume by night, his smile the kind people have when collecting their scoop at the casino.

He gave off repellent, excessive self-confidence; a trace of his previous job in senior management and the custom of losing money and then finding it again. But this appeared rather attractive. He was much like a broken business owner, still having the habits of a wealthy person that he likes to gratify, with little weaknesses that were way too many and that he easily forgave himself for, like a guilty cat.

"I'll drop in at my friend's place. I realized that you are a bookkeeper a bit later. When I told you I was under investigation, you became somewhat interested. Are you still interested? Could we have a cup of coffee at your place?"

"I'm not a bookkeeper, but an assistant investigator. Neither are you; you are not a bookkeeper – not at all. You must be an ex-broker currently employed by a private security agency. So, haven't you changed your mind regarding coffee, yet?"

"A broker?"

"You never really waste your time," she prompted.

"I agree." And he gave her a nod, as if she'd just bought him.

"I have not been really talking you into this," she gave him a gentle smile.

"Um, so you may start doing it now. The clock's ticking."

Wednesday 23rd, 11.00 p.m.

Hoffmann arrived all of a sudden, with no previous call.

He said that he'd dropped in at Schumann's place and found a gunman there, who must have taken Hoffmann for Schumann's bodyguard. Hoffmann was able to put him down, and now this man was being handled by the police. The man was not so young: he wore a dark blue duffle coat and a red scarf, and had neither documents nor keys on him. Who would ever walk around the city with neither bank cards nor keys?

Hoffmann was lucky to have entered right after that gunman, and he'd happened to stand very close behind his back at the time when the man hit him, so Hoffmann slanted backward and, after getting a blow on his shoulder, found himself again right behind the man's back, so he'd managed to knock the man off balance. Naturally, Hoffmann had no handcuffs with him, and he asked Schumann to bring him something solid, so the latter brought him some lady's stockings. Hoffmann thought better of calling the police and brought the gunman to the police station in person.

I suddenly thought that I might lose Hoffmann, and this was scary. Catching my eye, he asked me,

"Do you come to fancy me now? I've bought you some mini cakes."

"Yes. I'd love to have a mini cake."

Thinking of those mini cakes... Where could we be now, with Vlad if Ernest had not brought us here? We did not really know where to go. Hoffmann, by a strange coincidence, had become our only safeguard. Why were we here? Could he know something else? Or, otherwise... And I thought, *At night, everything will look different again.* The words would be filled with a different meaning, the spill of light from the neighborhood windows would die out, and the darkness would stick onto the glass. In the chilly air, every noise from the calming-down highway would echo like glass, and by morning it would all die off; but I would be able to still hear the breath of the cooling-off city behind the window. No, I had no wish to run away from here, really; but what if it was a fairy tale about Hansel and Gretel?

"Could you make us coffee; would you be so kind?" Hoffmann requested, and then reached for his cell.

"I've been telling you not to let him out... What, his apologies? No, I cannot accept his fucking apologies... Yes, I understand, he's been so nice."

After having this talk, Hoffmann hung up,

"He's gone now. He turned out to be a bookkeeper, in fact. A guy with a bear hug... can you believe it?" Hoffmann turned to Vlad and then shrank with pain at a touch to his own shoulder.

"Ernest, you've got to see a doctor..." and I cut myself short right away. His glance was like a wall on which I could clearly read the message to take away all that courtesy.

"Uh-huh, could you hide away that caring look of yours?" he specified, giving another grimace of pain.

Ernest said that the gunman had been taken over by the counsel at law, Richter, who'd brought all his paperwork. "The bookkeeper" had told them he feared so much for his life that he'd arranged for a lawsuit against himself, and he'd explained that it appeared safer for him to be under investigation in Dusseldorf than stay in Moscow. His case had been linked to some never-ending Russian story regarding money laundering, and there had been a coincidence of names. The lawyer would have paid a fine for him; nothing else. According to "the bookkeeper," he'd run away from his attendant because he'd taken a liking to a woman. He would have returned of his own accord...

"...and he was almost back, but he kind of got lost, fucking hell, in this unknown city, by entering a wrong building; and then he took me for a Russian who, as it seemed to him, must have found him there. The man was ready to bring his apologies to me and also to Schumann. And then he was so very nice, as per the female assistant investigator with whom he must have had time to fuck over on his way to Schumann's place. Complete fuck-up," Hoffmann concluded. "He must have disappeared by now. Yet another runaway accountant. If I had known, I would have crushed his ribs so that he would linger in the clinic a bit longer. I could be listening to his apologies ad infinitum. Something tells me that this is not the last bookkeeper on the way. And for some reason, I don't give a damn about Schumann." Ernest grumbled, now back to his own thoughts, and then he said to Vlad, "There are way too many duplicates; even the crazy Russians never do it that way, that's not their style. Don't you think so? There must be someone odd in there; a duplicate of his own self. So who are you, you sonofabitch?"

"Alexander Schulz, a bank robber," Vlad responded merrily.

Wednesday 23rd, 11.45p.m.

Hoffmann left and Vlad and I had some more vodka, sitting there waiting for the fireplace wood to burn to ashes.

"Why did he come to Schumann? Was it to ask him whether Schumann was paid to Leman, or for the latter to tell he was paid by Blatt? That sounds doubtful." I did not really know what to think, going over all those events in my mind again as if they were puzzle pieces fallen apart.

"There is something we don't know about Schumann," Vlad agreed.

As a matter of fact, the whole thing had started from the lawsuit against the banker Schumann, a former intern in the audit company where Vlad used to work at a certain point in time under his true surname Smith. Could we have missed something in there? But what else could we think if Schumann, this motherfucker, actually looked like a hundred percent banker while his bank was the size of ...a laundry room? Wasn't it weird that a banker had started buying out all those old personal data files? True, he might have bought them out; but was he really able to keep them a secret? We believed it was much better to have these files destroyed, and Schumann must have done it, but we never believed he could have been doing it disinterestedly. We actually believed that all those agents were supposed to fulfill a single task. That is, might they have been contacting Schumann in a certain way? And did he really have no fears while living that way, as a walking vault?

One day I realized that Vlad, with the full list of partners on his hands, was a sort of a walking vault. However, Vlad was ready for everything. And what about Schumann? He was a regular banker.

"Yes, indeed, why was this Schumann the man to have bought out those personal data files? He's been doing it on his own. How could he be so fearless?

They can actually approach him to find out the names of those agents. In such cases, they never really choose the means. And then, he is a banker..."

"I got it," Vlad said, tipping back in his armchair.

"What?"

"Schumann must have bought out his own data file in the first place."

"That is, that bookkeeper without paperwork is one of the people whose case files he must have bought out?"

"Yes. He must not have come not to kill Schumann, or to have a talk with him. He must have come to ask him what to do next... to do with whom?..." Vlad froze to the spot with this guess. "With Ivan? Or Blatt? Or with me?"

Like this book?

Maybe you leave a review?

LIE MAKES ME LIVE

Book Five of The Sleeper Series

by Anna Schlegel

Coming soon

This game of the intelligence, we were either to see through it, or die.

There is an old brain teaser about three different gods, God of Lie, God of Truth and God of Chance. One of them lied all the time, another told everyone the truth only, and the third one could either tell the truth or lie. So who of them was who in there?

Who was that man? There happened to be three people who had told they knew the man. So who of them could be telling the truth? And who must have been lying?

Who could have been led up the path? And what kind of person was he himself? He was the only man to know the answer, but he was the God of Lie.

You may wish to learn a bit more about the legendary agent, and these books would most likely catch your eye. Will you be able to find within them the answer to the question of whether Philby was indeed a legendary spy? I doubt it.

A Spy Among Friends: Kim Philby and the Great Betrayal

by Ben Macintyre, John le Carré

To my mind, it's a better idea to read Phillip Knightley. He starts his book from the point when he stepped across the threshold of Kim Philby's apartment in Moscow. This book has an answer.

Philby: KGB Mastermind

by Phillip Knightley

I'm writing about Kim Philby from a different side; that is, from the side where he used to be loved, and where he remains as a living legend.

From Russia with love,

Anna Schlegel

MONEY CAN'T LIE

Book One of The Sleeper Series
by Anna Schlegel

ISBN: 9780998185347
ASIN: B01M1BZR1X

Should there be three pieces of crap this is of the British intelligence classic.

He was not worth a straw to Intelligence; he was a mere sleeper, just a small coin. One day he felt that behind his back there was someone else; someone a big shot of such high value that they could not afford to lose him. Who could that be, – a recent defector? He had no idea.

He could only sense a trace of him, barely-there, just a nip. They were seeking to ward off the trail, and not just by drawing it aside. Now it appeared to lead straight to him. Every little thing pointed to him.

The trace would be lifeless, classically beautiful and as such stone-dead.

WHO SPREADS FOR WHOM
Book Two of The Sleeper Series

by Anna Schlegel

ISBN: 9780998185385
ASIN: B06WLGZ444

The British Intelligence cannot compromise its integrity; it will adhere to its principles like in the old times of rock 'n roll. And it's damn good to see it working... but then, it's scary to see it work against you.

They seemed to be looking for a perfect witness for that legal action. One was a sleeper, another a dead sleeper, and the third was a dummy agent. While this man alone passed for all three, he was never summoned to court.

THE GODS SMILE ON THE BASTARDS

Book Three of The Sleeper Series

by Anna Schlegel

ISBN: 9780998185392
ASIN: B06XYVGTK6

Once you are able to see intelligence's hand, you may see the words of failure inscribed in the same handwriting - a failure they are yet unaware of.

By looking at that other man from afar, he found it hard to shake off the feeling of looking at his own self from the outside. That other man resembled him way too much. The man was better than him, more experienced and farfetched, and he looked more convincing, and rather a slime ball. Everyone could see it. The man succeeded in making everyone around believe he was truly him, in person. And the man could prove it. What would eventually happen if the man slipped off? Then the only guy remaining there would be himself. And he would be constrained to be more like his former self. For all those long years, he had plain forgotten what kind of person he was underneath. He would have to recollect this and become somewhat more life-like. He would hardly be able to make it, really, unless he was dead. But then, would it be a preferable option - something they truly wanted?

Why do intelligence people become turncoats? There may be two answers. One is obvious. They become turncoats due to a landmark case against other turncoats. Every agent, while keeping a close watch on the case, usually dissects the defendant's mistakes, so he thinks he would never do anything similar; that he could do things smarter, with a lot more caution...

The second answer is something else. People come to be turncoats long before they start working for the spy directorate. So read it all: this is worth knowing. This is the answer from a legend. Listen to it, give it a touch, and you'll be blessed with a smile of God.

ABOUT THE AUTHOR

Why do I know so much of the Intelligence? It must have come from between the bed sheets, and not just this much. Victor returned to Moscow after a few years of work as a financial expert. He was more of a moneyman than a special service agent, even more he was a swindler. He became a raider like so many others, during those years. He used to have both good luck and failure in bank seizures, in which he lost money. I imperceptibly turned to be just the same like him.

These books are written from an adventurer's perspective. There are no good guys, since those good guys have no chance of attracting a female. Women want bastards.

Why read my books? I've got the undeniable strength of being a Russian author, which means that I'm writing about the Russian Intelligence without using much fiction.

Of course, these are just mere fiction novels, a kind of multi-twist mind game; yet I'm describing events the way they could have touched me in reality. So these books actually represent my "might-have-been" by seizing the fact that I could have lived a number of alternative lives. Understandably, one life is enough for me: my behind would hardly stand more adventures. I'm writing about things that I find interesting. I've only read a few books of spy fiction - for the most part, they are deadly boring.

I was born in Moscow. I studied at the Moscow State University at the Philosophical facility. I got a PhD in philosophy and stayed without work and without money. The financial crisis began. Some years I looked for a work, but took it easy. I became a securities trader in an investment company by chance. And then came the default in 1998. I was without work again.

This was my best time. I became the financial middleman for off-market private transactions. I had nothing. I had been looking for too-big deals. But then there was a time when it was quite possible for me to be the middleman in the sale of a Libyan oil tanker or for the sale of an aircraft abroad. I got sick of conducting multi-million dollar transactions and lost all sense of reality.

I met Victor. Capturing the bank was in my sights. The insider of the bank was its vice-president. I write about his capture almost verbatim. Before leaving, he gave me his three passports... So I do not know his real name. There were no closed doors for him. He had friends from the federal agency for government communication and information from the board of directors of Deutsche Bank. All kinds of people.

Years passed. Victor is long gone. And there are fewer middlemen.

I feel myself to be on the way out. My whole generation is on the way out as well; those who are described as robbing the country.

I like those who robbed the country, and I'm pleased about how it was done. They were really talented financiers; nothing worse than the financiers on Wall Street. They left the country and took the money with them.

Since then, Moscow's air did not smell of millions any longer. But, it seemed to me, it was still in the depths of my house between a pile of white shirts. Now there are no more financial middlemen. The young have gotten jobs first. They receive a salary at the end of the month, and seem to have already forgotten the smell of crazy millions. It's like being drunk. There's a dizziness from it ... They did not want to breathe this air. They did not want to poison their lives. They earned their money. They had wives, children, dogs, and cars, which it was necessary to care of... Their heads have overflowed with thoughts of petty cash.

Then the middlemen were old. And I stayed with them. Therefore, the heroes of my novels are in their sixties. To the former friends who stayed in the stock market, I became infected. No, I just died. And I smell of sweet cadaveric decay. It seemed to me that I was among the dead. And it felt really bad for me, as a living being. But I shared their way of thinking. I was the same as they were: ridiculous and old-fashioned, useless clutter, rubbish. Market garbage. My friends were precisely the same as middle-aged gentlemen.

Sometimes I catch a strange look directed towards me, but then forget about it. The metropolis wiped me from their memory. There was no need to be as nice as kind people who talk with clients and colleagues daily. I had a different way of talking. My talking always led to a deal. And if it didn't, I would give the finger and immediately forget the useless person, as if shaking off dust. And that's all.

I have nothing to regret. I had nothing to blame

myself for. Dogs wouldn't blame themselves for their dog's life, would they?

I cannot return to the stock market. It has changed. Brokers, buyers, and sellers have been changed. They all grew up a little. They have got each other for 0.1 percent interest, ready to sell their ass to everyone at 0.5 percent, and would sell their own mother at one percent. I could not do that. The market has kicked me out as garbage.

And the old, among whom I used to be, are gone. The reality of small money has burned out people all around me as fire burns wood. Sometimes it seems to me that I have gone mad; that I live in a world turned inside out. Sometimes I would like to be like anyone... to have a rest, eat, dress, buy a car...

But I can't do it. It would be a living death.

It seems to me I would lose days and years and would end up in devastation and poverty. And I would lose the scent of money, and my skills ... so I clung to the sale of oil, diamonds, and bank guarantees, though I'm sure that it was simply thin air and there was nothing behind it. Sometimes I woke up and thought that all was not with me. But I lived and breathed the air of millions. It was my life. In my life, I gained money from thin air. Emptiness is a magnet for me.

Now I have got nothing. I do not care. I like my life. I like to go for millions. It's impossible to stop me. I might have to be put down like a mad dog.

And I still have a sense of money. I can smell the street's air and say that the market has changed. It smells as sharp as the smell of fresh bread from a bakery in the winter.

THE DEAD BANK DIARY SERIES

THE DEAD BANK DIARY
Book One of The Dead Bank Diary Series
ISBN: 9780986174919
ASIN: B00OPAZQMI

FOR THOSE IN THE SHADE
Book Two of The Dead Bank Diary Series
ISBN: 9780986174964
ASIN: B014Q92DE6

THE PRINTS ON THE SNOWS OF YESTERYEAR
Book Three of The Dead Bank Diary Series
ISBN: 9780986174988
ASIN: B017KYY2MA

SOME DAY I'LL HIT A BANK
Book Four of The Dead Bank Diary Series
ISBN: 9780998185323
ASIN: B01LYZ3XQX

THE FROZEN DEBT
Book Five of The Dead Bank Diary Series
ISBN: 9780998185309
ASIN: B01LX1AKZ7

AUTHOR'S NOTE

In these books there are no cops; no killings. There is much about the illegal takeover of banks, and a powerful amount of money. I know how to pump up a bank, and how to bankrupt one. I love beautiful gray schemes on the verge of being crimes. My stories are about fraud as seen through the eyes of a swindler. There are no good guys.

I write about the golden-time bankers from 1998, when neither the police nor the intelligence services, or any crimes, prevented the banks from making money.

These novels are not based on a true story, but you will face this reality in every word.

ABOUT THE DEAD BANK DIARY SERIES

These are stories about a man who is not alive anymore. He was a financier; a retired intelligence officer. I had the good luck to arrange a couple of financial frauds. We bumped into each other before the recession, in the flood of shit, and were together in the dust.

After his death, I still had the power of attorney.

Of course, Victor knew I wouldn't be able to work his contacts. I had tried. Now it's funny to think of it. I am, and have always been, a go-between; a rat. Nobody needs middlemen. They get rid of them; they send them to Hell. But I had a white shirt with a necktie and copies of million dollar contracts for oil, gas, diamonds, and rare-earth metals: light as air, rolled fax sheets with lots of zeroes. They made me giddy; they made me drunk. And I ran along with them, and easily foisted them onto the middlemen: muddy, middle-aged misters.

When some of the first deals failed, I went into hysterics. I wanted to throw in the towel.

Once I had a dream. In my dream, I listened to a telephone call: "Miss Schlegel? We need your signature to extend a contract concluded by Mr..."

I woke up scared; something turned over inside of me. I realized that I was spending my life waiting for such a call. It didn't matter where it caught me.

But there was no going back. Once you've taken a step forward, you realize you can't turn back anymore.

Why did he leave all this to me? I looked over the papers, recalling past years, deals, people, talks - everything from the first meeting to the last minute. And I couldn't find anything for me; because it wasn't for me, actually, but for the old me. So I changed. I became a con.

My life was changed. Sometimes it was as convincing and disgusting as the life of a whore. It was as inaccessible as the man who despises you. It was like vomit or sweat from the body from a heavy hangover's shivers. You wish to run, but there's no place to run to. It's a cold stupor. So it's stupid to look at the smeared corpse on the road, and it's impossible to regain consciousness to look away. This passion nests in the heart, and you don't know what it is.

I have his photo, the last one, taken at Arkhangelskoe hospital. Summer. We're sitting on the edge of a dried-up fountain. He embraces me with one arm, and I'm lost next to him. He is gray-haired and corpulent. He has a mocking look. And behind us there are towering white marble angels.

THE DEAD BANK DIARY

Book One of The Dead Bank Diary Series

by Anna Schlegel

ISBN: 9780986174919
ASIN: B00OPAZQMI

The rats living on the refuse of the bank's backyard stay full at all times

This is not a robbery. A bank is taken with all its guts: accounts, debts, points of exchange, the staff down to the last secretary, the building. This is beautiful and clean fraud.

I was out of work, while all around, you could smell millions even in the air outside. It was an unforgettable smell of public debt, oilfields, gold, bank guarantees, diamonds... I wanted to breathe in the air of easy cash Moscow, to revel and roll in this air. I could feel the smell of money in the wind on my face. This air was used to make up funds overnight; to make a fortune, go to rack and ruin, and then grow rich again. It was blowing freely across the wreckage of the sold-out Soviet empire.

I was asked to help redeem the debts of a bank. The insider man at the bank held the post of Vice President.

A bit of danger and a bit of love.

FOR THOSE IN THE SHADE

Book Two of The Dead Bank Diary Series

by Anna Schlegel

ISBN: 9780986174964
ASIN: B014Q92DE6

You may live your whole life without getting to know who
you are, and sometimes this is for the better

It was a bank robbery. However, this time the gunmen came not for the cash but for the bank itself, and all that followed happened faster than a domino knockdown.

The bank was bankrupted professionally.

Bad debts of the Third World countries, Cuba, Zimbabwe, Morocco, and The Congo, have been returned to the bank's balance sheet. Once, the bank sold the debts to itself; to an offshore company.

Who did this?

The banker finds the bank in Amsterdam... and has taken it over completely.

THE PRINTS ON THE SNOWS OF YESTERYEAR

Book Three **of** The Dead Bank Diary Series

by Anna Schlegel

ISBN: 9780986174988
ASIN: B017KYY2MA

The best one to rob the bank is the banker himself

The bank, facing bankruptcy, fell out of his hands like a snowball rolling downhill to flatten everything under its weight.

Behind every bankruptcy, there are people who make it happen. But there are no influential people. Big figures are absent. It seems you stay face to face with the emptiness.

This happens when the Central Bank is playing against you.

SOME DAY I'LL HIT A BANK

Book Four of The Dead Bank Diary Series

by Anna Schlegel

ISBN: 9780998185323
ASIN: B01LYZ3XQX

The bomb lives to its internal time

My life became lonely and monotonous, almost mechanical in nature, with a mechanism akin to a ticking bomb. It could be ticking for days and weeks, quiet and imperceptible, only to blow up everything around at the right time.

This is the way common folks used to live in the past; bakers and shoemakers. They lived their lives until the revolution burst out. It was their time. And then they went out the door of their bakery and shoe shop for good, to take the ministry chairs and cut the heads off the aristocracy by weaving plots and intrigues. I knew I would not miss my time.

It seemed to me I could go on for another ten years, only to one day stumble on a terse line in the newspaper and realize: my time has come.

THE FROZEN DEBT

Book Five of The Dead Bank Diary Series

by Anna Schlegel

ISBN: 9780998185309
ASIN: B01LX1AKZ7

When the totally nude have a look, maybe you still have the shoulder loops

One morning he stayed bare-ass. There was no money, no name, no wife, and nothing left... just his shoulder loops.

The deal Victor had set up six years ago kept running like clockwork and suddenly came to a halt. The accounts of the company formerly owned by Victor were blocked by the public prosecution. The man who found Victor in Moscow offered to give him everything back: his company and his board membership and ... his wife.

Upon his arrival in Berlin, Victor realized that all parties wanted a goner.

And Victor was an ideal goner, as he was also a mole.

Anna Schlegel has a degree in philosophy. She was a securities trader before the recession. For the last ten years she has been involved in off-market private transactions as a middleman in Moscow.

Anna lives in Novi Sad, Serbia.

CONTACTS INFORMATION

For information about the author, please visit TheSleeper.club

thedeadbankdiary@gmail.com

For information about the published books, please contact Schlegel Press Association at

schlegelpressassociation@gmail.com